# ACCUSATIONS

## ANGEL B.

BIG::DREAMS
PRODUCTION

## ACKNOWLEDGMENTS

I'd like to thank everyone that put up with me during the time it took for me to write this novel. I appreciate your input and support, and all the guidance that was given to me. Love you! Muah!

**Angel B.** is a native of New Jersey and loves wielding her characters around the different individuals she meets. She grew up the youngest in a large family of ten that was constantly filled with laughter, yet, had just as many moments of pain. She was raised in an era when drugs and disease hit her neighborhood hard, and her only escape was reading, and later writing. Taking heed to the advice from veteran author Treasure Blue, she found herself, adding small scenario's from her life into her books to connect on a personal level with her readers.

Her first book, Loving Rainy Days, was released in 2011 with great success and she has been wowing her readers with awesome novels ever since. She has been interviewed by Black Writers Space and has had an author spotlight done on her in the Literary Jewels Magazine in 2012. Joey Pinkney caught up with Angel B. for an interview in 2012 as well, and in 2013, Angel B. was an African American Literary Awards Show Nominees for best short story.

## Books By ANGEL B.

### The Tase Men Series
Loving Rainy Days Vol. 1
Michael's Heat Vol. 2
Up For The Chase Vol. 3

Child Support
Unstable Creature
The 7$^{th}$ Commandment (Novelette)

### I Must Be Crazy Series (Short Story)
My Masked Lover Episode 1
Teacher's Pet Episode 2
Daily Dose Episode 3

Visit Angel's Website at
www.freeyourmindtobooks.com
Facebook
www.facebook.com/AngelBearfield
Amazon Central
amazon.com/author/angelbearfield

# Chapter 1

The Silver two-door Mercedes pulled in front of the tall building that sat on the corner of Alameda just north of the 101. The Silver two-door Mercedes pulled in front of the tall building that sat on the corner of Alameda just north of the 101. Terri Powell loved being close to the highway so that she was not too far from downtown. That way at the end of her busy day she had a straight shot towards home. It had taken her two years of marketing and a stern business acumen to get her off Slauson Avenue and into a respectable area that she knew would make her clients feel comfortable about hiring her.

She pulled into the underground garage as she commandeered her normal parking spot that was less than three feet from the entrance. Why not? She owned the building.

She did a once over of the parking spots near her own looking to see if Malik's Porsche was there. Usually, his work hard lifestyle would persuade him to play even harder every weekend, and Terri had become used to him being at least an hour late on Mondays. However, this past year he has made a complete three sixty, and has been coming in on time. She knew that he would be sauntering in shortly heading to the coffee pot to make his extra strong black mix with nine packs of Nutra Sweet.

Terri stepped out of the car, letting her long sleek legs cross one by one. You could see the muscles in her calves flex under her smooth glossy skin. Looking at her, she made it obvious that light years measured distance and not time, seeing that she was an ageless beauty.

Grabbing her Coach satchel that held her laptop, she headed for the elevator. The *V Tower* was the home of other lucrative businesses that she leased to, but her main concern was her own company, *Vows*, which was slowly climbing up the Forbes list as being one of the best companies of the year. She wasn't ready to start shoveling out stock options, but she was ecstatic that they compared her in another article in Black Enterprise as the Black Martha Stewart.

Stepping on the elevator, she pushed the number ten button sending her to where she had totally remodeled the entire floor to fit her personality. The red leather couches and glass décor is what greeted her clients in the outer office. The white carpeting throughout the suite kept the place bright and vibrant. Although Vows took up the entire floor, it only consisted of a large sitting area, board room, front desk greeting area with a full assistant desk, and of course her own office which included a full apartment attached through an adjoining door. The colors blended perfectly together and Terri loved the feeling of success she felt every time she walked through the doors.

The elevator stopped, and Terri stepped off and unlocked the glass door. The first thing she did was spray the place down with her favorite Jasmine scent before she entered her private office. It only took seconds before the phone started to ring and she had to answer knowing that it would be a little longer before Malik arrived.

"Vows," she said as she placed her satchel on the desk.

"Hello, is this the place that saves marriage's?" the voice on the other end asked.

Terri smiled before responding. "I would certainly like to think so. My name is Terri Powell. I'm the owner of Vows. How can I help you?"

"I hope you can help me. My name is Lilah. Lilah Thompson."

"Very pretty name," Terri said. "Now tell me what seems to be the problem in your marriage?" she continued as she heard a door open from outside her office.

"Well, first of all, Sean and I aren't married just yet. He's my fiancé. However, we're supposed to be getting married in August. It just seems like something has changed about him. Sean is usually very jovial and outgoing, but lately he has been acting a little...indifferent," said Lilah.

"I see," Terri replied, taking some notes on her little note pad. "May I ask what your fiancés name is?"

"Oh, I'm sorry. It's Sean Clemens."

Terri thought the name sounded very familiar; maybe a celebrity. She wasn't a stranger to celebrity clients and had once teamed up with the producers of the popular reality show *Cheaters* to help a young couple try and keep their marriage together. She'd agreed to have one of her employees make an attempt for the husbands attention and the show had loved the results.

Now she was on the phone with a new client listening to her explain her reasons for feeling that something wasn't right with her fiancé. One thing about Terri was that she was a very good listener. It was one of her strong points and she always figured that she could learn more about the client by letting them talk. So after listening to Lilah explain why she needed her services, she told her the fee that Vows charged, and it was settled.

Terri sat back in her oversized leather chair and thought about her own life. Every time she took on a new client, it made her think about why she chose to do this as a career. She was much like the women who had just called. Long ago she had lost her trust in men herself when her own father left home without any warnings. *Fifteen years of marriage gone. He didn't even say goodbye to me,* she thought sadly.

She remembered that day like it was yesterday. She could still see herself standing at the top of the stairs in their home listening to her mother beg her father not to go. He had been having an affair with a

4

woman from San Diego. It had been going on even before they had married.

Terri had been fourteen at the time that the separation had taken place. She was at that age where the boys were starting to take an interest in her. They were asking her for her phone number at school and tossing compliments her way. She hated her father knowing that she wasn't going to learn from him what to look out for when it came to boys. Instead, what she learned from him was how men would pretend to love you to get what they wanted before leaving you high and dry. She got to witness that first hand and the humiliating response from her mother.

*"No, Wesley, it doesn't have to be like this. Please baby, we have a family, and we need you," her mother pleaded.*

*"Look Gail, it's finished. This has gone on long enough. I'm not in love with you. As a matter of fact, I was never in love with you. This marriage has only been a career move for me," he replied. "Thanks to your father's connections I was able to move up through the company quickly. But, I don't need you guys any longer. Hell, I only stayed around this long for the kid. But she's practically grown so I'm leaving. Don't bother trying to call. I left the cell on the bed."*

He didn't know that Terri was standing there listening. Nor did he care. He caught a glimpse of her at the top of the stairs, and with not so much as a smile in her direction, turned and walked out the door with just the clothes on his back.

That was 14 years ago, and now at 28, Terri had capitalized on the one thing her father had given her, the ingenious design that Vows was built on. Men and women alike would pay a huge fee to know before, and even after they had tied the knot, if they could truly trust their significant other to be faithful. Somehow she felt that if her mother had put her father to the test before she said 'I do' she would have seen through his pathetic little lie of love.

Thankfully, her mother only sulked around for a few weeks. After having a conversation with her father, she began working for him in the finance department. It was there, two years later, that she met Donald Porter. He was a client and had asked her out several times before she had given in and said yes. They had dated three years before they were married. Today, they are still happily married and living in Miami.

Malik stood in Terri's office doorway watching her. She was gazing out the window totally caught up in her daydream. He smiled at the pensive look that caused her perfectly arched eyebrows to draw together. Usually she would have noticed him by now, but she must be thinking about something heavy today.

He remembered the first time he saw her standing over by the large windows in the conference room. She had been giving interviews for a personal assistant that wouldn't mind doing a little socializing outside of the office and he knew that he would be perfect for the job.

However, his interest in the position had been forgotten once he stepped into the room and saw the shapely beauty standing there with the light from the sun bringing out the deep shine of her hair. His gaze had dropped to her shoulders and down to her plump backside, and stayed there. As he was looking down at her ass in the short skirt he remembered thinking, *'damn, I hope she's not the boss.'*

And now, after three years of working together and being friends, he was lost because he now felt something more. Sometimes he thought she felt something as well, but then there were times when he thought he was wrong. The one thing he did know was that if she did feel something, he would be ready for whatever. That's why he had stopped club hopping and had even stopped dating. It was as if he had his life on hold waiting for her. *And she's absolutely worth the wait*, he thought, smiling in her direction.

Shaking his head at her lack of attention to her surroundings, he began waving his hand from side to side to jog her back to reality. "Are you thinking about me again?" he asked in his deep baritone.

Malik always showed up for work prepared, looking and smelling like he was ready for a photo shoot. Women couldn't stay away from his tall honey complexioned body. His strong wide shoulders, muscled physique, and beautiful features, were enough to cause women to throw propriety to the wind, and everything they were wearing.

Terri glanced over at him standing in the doorway and smiled. *Hell, the man was a gift of temptation all wrapped up in a sexy bow. And I want one.*

7

"Actually, I *was* thinking about you. I need you to pull up everything you can on Sean Clemens," she replied, handing him the name written on a sticky note.

"Thee, Sean Clemens, the boxer?" Malik asked.

"I guess so," she said not having a clue about him, or boxing for that matter. "Now get to work," she said jokingly.

Malik smiled and saluted her like a soldier. "Yes, Mam," he said and headed towards his desk.

## Chapter 2

Malik sat at his desk punching keys on his computer with lightning speed. He loved his job very much and loved the fact that it permitted him so much freedom. Another reason he liked his job was because it allowed him to work closely with Terri. He had been working for Vows now for three years and there wasn't a night that went by that he didn't dream of her lying next to him in his loft apartment. Since she had no idea how he felt about her, it was his own secret hell to bear.

Focusing back on work, Malik Googled, checked Facebook, Instagram, and Twitter, compiling any information that was relevant to their new client's case, based on Sean Clemens. The only information that he found was the normal stuff that was on everybody's social media sites. That's what made Malik suspicious though. One thing about Malik is that he had an eye for seeing things most people would overlook, and there was definitely something going on.

He quickly typed in the three w's and punched in the word paparazzinow.com behind them. It was a secure site that only allowed individuals of an elite society in as members. He made it to the home page, typed in his password, and logged on. When he navigated to the sports figure tab, he typed in Sean's name.

"Ahhhh, just as I suspected. A punching bag isn't the only thing this pretty boy is hitting these days," Malik said to himself and clicked the button to print out the photos.

He read the name of the photographer who took the photo's and saw that it was someone that they'd worked with on numerous occasions. It didn't hurt either that he was also a good friend of his. Quickly, Malik dialed Thomas's number on his cell. Thomas picked up on the first ring.

"Well, if it isn't the Vows boy," he said, recognizing the number.

"Shut the hell up Thomas and tell me what you know about this Sean Clemens character," Malik replied smiling.

Thomas laughed. "Beside him having a mean right hook, man I can say this. That cat's into some real heavy shit. That gym he owns ain't nothing more than a sleaze bag after hour spot for boy on boy shit," said Thomas sounding sickened to even repeat it.

"Thanks, I owe you one," said Malik. He wasn't surprised about what Thomas had said, especially after he had visited the website and saw him posing in many suspect looking photos.

"I'll take floor seats to the next Clipper's game,"

Thomas responded laughing before ending the call.

Malik jumped up, snatched the photos and the information he'd printed out from the tray of the printer and stuffed it inside a manila envelope. He then headed back to Terri's office. She was on a call and held her index finger up to signal him to give her a second. He stood there in front of her desk watching her speak on the phone. Her lightly glossed lips smiled at something the person on the phone said, and Malik felt his chest tighten.

Terri was beautiful, and that was putting it mildly. She was in spectacular shape with a killer body, dressed like a runway model, and always held herself like a lady. Most men should feel fortunate just to be in her presence. *Hell, I know I do*, Malik thought to himself.

Terri ended her call and gave Malik her undivided attention. "Okay, big boy, lay it on me," she said, flashing a big white smile and rubbing her hands together in anticipation of the information he must have found on Clemens.

*Big boy is right*, he thought to himself smirking. "You're not going to believe this," Malik replied, taking one of the chairs in front of her desk.

"Coming from you, and your million ways to obtain information, I think anything is believable," she chided.

Malik smiled at her words which were meant to be a compliment, not an insult. "I'll start by saying your plan A might not be such a good idea. We might have to use plan B," Malik insisted.

Her smile faltered as she watched him from behind her desk. "Come again," she said, not understanding.

"Let's just say you're not a contender to get in the ring with Mr. Clemens. Now if you call that fancy dressing guy that's always getting his eyebrows arched, you'll have a much better chance at getting the information we need."

Terri laughed. "I take it you mean Andre Harper?" she asked with amusement. Malik might not agree with Andre's lifestyle, but they got along just fine.

"Exactly. Andre is more his speed," Malik replied standing up. "Have a look," he said and tossed the folder he held in his hands on her desk that was filled with the information he'd found on Sean before bouncing up and returning to his own office.

Terri opened the folder and looked at the pictures of Sean and hoped that for the first time in three years that Malik was wrong. It sure was going to be a waste of a good man if the information was correct. Beside's that, the poor girl that called to hire her would obviously be devastated.

It was still early, and even though she valued Malik's Intel, Terri decided to still take the first crack at Sean. She didn't want to send in Harper and it all turned out to be a mistake. So, in order to leave no stone left unturned, she would go on with plan A. If Sean doesn't bite, only then would she move on to plan B. She smiled, remembering she had a workout bag in her office closet.

"Guess this old body can use a little Stairmaster in its life," she said to herself.

Terri walked from behind her desk and opened the closet, and there it was. Her Nike bag contained her white leggings, and a turquoise fitted body suit that was sure to captivate any man. That was if that man was into women. She grabbed the bag and hit the intercom button on her phone.

"Malik, hold all my calls for the rest of the day, and locate Andre Harper in case you're right."

"So you're still going to give it a try, huh?" asked Malik. Terri heard the humor in his voice and couldn't help smiling.

"I guess it's the only way to truly find out, right?" she responded, still standing by the phone.

"Suit yourself, but are you going to wear that turquoise number?" he asked, feeling a little jealous. Malik was thinking back to the days when they would go downstairs and work out together at the gym that opened on the second floor. Terri looked like a black Bay Watch beauty in that little turquoise one piece.

"Right you are again," she responded, ending the call.

Terri was heading out her office when the entrance door to Vows was swung open wide. A young woman charged inside, dragging a little girl behind her. The child was holding on to a naked doll tightly as if her life depended on it.

"Where the hell is your boss?" she yelled. Her question was directed at Malik, but when she saw

Terri she made a beeline for her. Terri dropped the bag she was holding ready to defend herself if need be.

The woman let her daughter's hand go and balled her fist in anger. "This is all your fault," she yelled in a rage. "You ruined my damn marriage. My life."

Malik jumped up from behind his desk and stood between the woman and Terri. "Mrs. Pierre, calm down." Although he was trying to calm the woman, he'd be damned if he let her put her hands on Terri.

"Calm down! How can I calm down after what she did?"

"Mrs. Pierre, I didn't do anything to you. You paid me to do a job and I did. I gave you the information we came by after doing the job and then you are left with making the decision afterwards of whether to stay or leave. Now I told you that your fiancé was cheating on you relentlessly. He failed every test I threw at him countless times. I then informed you of this, and showed you physical evidence, yet you still chose to marry him. That was your choice not mine. So do not come in here yelling and screaming about it being my fault."

Mrs. Pierre stood there silently, then suddenly began to bawl crazily. Malik drew back looking at Terri in alarm. Terri shoulders dropped with sympathy. She looked over at Malik and the little girl, and after seeing the horror on both of their faces, knew she had to get Mrs, Pierre somewhere secluded.

"Malik why don't you get Saniya a juice from the

break room while I have a talk with Mrs. Pierre."

Looking relieved that he could be somewhere else other than listening to the horrible racking sounds coming from the woman, he turned around and scooped the little girl up in his arms and headed for the small break room.

After they left, Terri grabbed Mrs. Pierre's hand and pulled her into her office. Ashley Pierre had come into Vows almost a year ago wanting to prove to her family that her fiancé Ramon Pierre, was fit to marry. Ramon Pierre was a big time party planner for LA's elite. Needless to say, within two weeks time, Ramon had been filmed and photographed with numerous woman. He had even agreed to sleep with Terri, showing up at the hotel and stripping naked. He was filmed jerking off in front of her, before she excused herself, and left the room.

When Terri issued all of this information to Ashley, she chose to ignore it, saying that he was only sowing his wild oats before getting married. Terri never makes any decisions for her clients. She delivers information, and then lets them make their own choices, whether to stay in the relationship or not. Now Ashley had made the wrong decision and was trying to blame Terri for it.

"Sit down Ashley," Terri instructed. She crossed the room over to the bar and poured her a glass of water. She placed three ice cubes in the glass and then brought it over to her.

Ashley took the glass with shaking hands. "Thank you."

Terri sat down beside her, not taking the chair behind her desk. By the way Ashley looked, with her wrinkled clothes and unkempt hair, she looked like she could use a friend.

"Ashley, what's going on? Tell me what happened?"

Tears began to stroll down her face, but this time there was no loud crying. Just silence. "You were right. I should have taken all the evidence that you'd given me and left his ass alone." She looked at Terri in anger and pain. "Do you know what he did?" she asked, not really wanting an answer. "He cheated on me."

Ashely shook her head. "But not with just some random ass chick. He…he fucked my damn sisters. All three of them," she said through clenched teeth. "That motherfucker slept with my sisters," she repeated as if she couldn't wrap her head around it. "In my house and in my bed."

Terri closed her eyes briefly. She knew there were no words that could console Ashley or have her relate to how she was feeling. So she just sat there and let her vent.

Ashley turned and looked over at Terri. "Do you know what that feels like. To know that the man that you love and share your body with intimately was sticking his dick in your sisters. Your own flesh and blood." She gave a harsh laugh. "Blood. That shit is a cliché. They were supposed to be my family. The ones that I could trust, you know? But in the end, my family fucked my man and got pregnant."

"Oh shit." Terri covered her hand with her mouth. She hadn't meant to let the outburst slip past her lips.

"Yeah, oh shit is right. My oldest sister is now pregnant by my husband. She's having a boy." Ashley shook her head in disgust. "That means Saniya's cousin will also be her little brother. How the hell am I supposed to explain that to her?"

Ashley tears continued to flow until she had none left. Terri sat quietly beside her as she stared down into the glass of water she held. As if she just realized where she was, her head lifted and she glanced over at Terri as if she hadn't known she was there.

"Oh, im sorry Ms. Powell. I didn't mean to drift off like that. I should get going. Saniya has a piano lesson and I have to get home and…"

When she stopped Terri reached over and squeezed her hand.

"I don't know what to do," said Ashley, looking dazed. "I mean, the house is his, and the cars."

"The first thing you need to do is make sure whatever you want to do won't hurt Saniya. She should be your main concern. All the materialistic things come second. So to keep Saniya happy, safe, and well taken care of, what should you do?"

Ashley sat there for a moment thinking, and then for the first time since walking into Vows, she smiled.

"I want a divorce. I'm going to file the papers after I drop off Saniya."

"Remember your contract with Vows. You can't use any of the information we've given you to help in your case," said Terri.

When Ashley's smile dropped, Terri went on. "Besides, you married him after receiving that information, so it's obsolete. You're divorcing him for violating his vows by committing adultery, right?"

Ashley smiled and then it widened into a full grin. "Yes, you're right. That's exactly right. And when I show that he even got my sister pregnant, there ain't a judge in this state that won't sympathize with me."

Terri smiled. "Exactly. Now come with me," Terri said, walking towards a door near the back of her office. She opened the door and stepped aside.

Ashley peeked inside and saw that it was a half bathroom. "What's this for?"

"So you can wash your face and fix your hair," she said frowning with a smirk. "Don't you ever come outside looking like this again. You almost gave me a heart attack."

Ashley looked in the mirror and cringed. "Damn." Her hair was all over the place, her lipstick smeared, and her mascara had been washed away leaving black striped down her cheeks.

"Damn is right," said Terri laughing. "Everything you'll need is in that closet behind you." Terri was about to close the door, then stopped. "Oh, and one more thing. Never break down like that in front of your daughter. She needs to know that you will forever be her rock, and after seeing you like this today, she might not be so sure of it anymore. When you're done, you might want to reassure her."

Ashley nodded. "Thanks for everything Ms. Powell."

"No problem, and call me Terri."

After Ashley got herself together, she came out and collected her daughter from Malik. She looked a lot calmer after their conversation, and even more so now that she had a plan.

"What did she tell you?" asked Malik. He stood next to her at the front entrance after saying their goodbyes to Ashley.

"He cheated on her."

"Oh," said Malik dryly.

"With her sisters."

He turned to look at her in disbelief. "Are you serious?"

"Yeah," said Terri, walking over to pick up her gym bag still intending to get to Sean Clemens gym. "He slept with all three of them."

"Get outta here," he said in shock.

When Terri reached the door, she stopped and looked over her shoulder. "He got the older sister pregnant."

Malik's mouth dropped open wide. "Oh shit!"

"Yeah, that's what I said," Terri said shaking her head. "Well, I'm off. I'll talk to you later," she said, stepping through the door. She gave him a quick wave before she disappeared down the hall.

## Chapter 3

Inside The Clemens Gym was incredible. It had
all the state of the art fitness equipment neatly
scattered throughout the facility with heated floors,
and a huge indoor swimming pool. There were wall
to ceiling mirrors everywhere and certified
employees walking around assisting the gym
members.

Terri changed in the women's locker room, which
also impressed her. Each locker had a built in retina
scan that served as a lock. A person would enter a
code, scan their pupil, and the only way that
particular locker would be opened again was if that
person scanned their eye again. She thought about
her security design for Vows, and knew that she
could have used Sean's imagination when having her
system designed.

There were numerous women in the facility
getting their workout on. A lot of them tall and
shapely and very gorgeous. Every one of them that
she looked at had Hollywood banging bodies making
Terri feel like she really needed to step her game up.
She knew she was a catch, but since she hadn't

worked out or dieted like she normally did, she had added on about seven unwanted pounds. It still didn't stop the men from eye molesting her gluteal region, but she didn't want to feel like she had too big of an ass.

Her first attack on her body was going to be the treadmill. She would set it on an easy incline and take it at a moderate pace. When Terri stepped on the machine, she looked at herself in the mirror as the belt began to move, causing her to keep pace or slide off. She was still fly to the nines, and felt that she looked just as good as any one of these women walking around with their own tight fitting numbers on.

The girl next to her was sweating profusely as her machine ran at a fast pace and a higher incline than Terri's. She could hear Joe's song, *I Wanna Know* blaring from the headphones that draped over the woman's head. For a moment she decided to speed up her machine, then thought better of it. *This is not a competition Girl. This machine will toss my ass on the floor and I'll end up on Facebook somewhere.*

Suddenly, Terri caught a glimpse of Sean through the mirror walking by, and followed him with her eyes. He surely was a good looking man with cream colored skin, smooth wavy hair, and strong shoulders. She could see the muscles protruding through his fitted workout gear and thought that Malik had to be wrong about his information.

She stopped the treadmill, grabbed her water bottle, and headed toward the weight room where she figured he'd gone. When Terri walked into the room, the smell of men sweating penetrated her nose and she felt a little something stir inside of her. As she observed all the different shades of incredible hulks tossing around iron like pancakes, she began looking for the one she'd come especially to see.

After a second she spotted Sean standing behind a bench spotting for another man who was attempting to lift what looked like all the weight in the world. Terri was in luck. The lightweights were right next to the bench the two men were at and she went over and lifted two twenty-pound dumbbells.

She started doing curls with the heavy instruments, and thought to herself that whoever decided to call the things dumbbells were right. *These damn things are heavy.* Her biceps were starting to ache and she wanted to quit, but knew that she had a job to do. Terri grunted as she counted to twenty and just as she was about to give up, she heard a voice behind her.

"Those look a little heavy for you," Sean said.

"So what are you trying to say? A woman can't be competitive," she replied smiling. *Grunt pant.*

Sean laughed at her comeback. "No, I'm not trying to say that at all my sista. I've been doing this a long time and I just wanted to tell you that it's not about the amount of weight you lift, but it's about the rep's you can crank out."

"Okay, Hercules, what makes you such a specialist?" she asked, pretending she didn't know him. She began checking out his light gray eyes and feeling a little mesmerized for a second.

"I'm Sean Clemens the owner, and I've been doing this for quite some time," he said extending a hand.

His voice was smooth, a little too much tenor for her liking, but that still didn't mean that Malik was right. Terri placed the weights back in their place on the rack, then turned to take his hand.

"Oh, so you do know what you're talking about. It's been a long time since I've actually worked out. I just figured since I have a wedding to go to in a few months I might as well get my dress size in order."

Terri smiled. She had seen the distraught look on his face when she mentioned the wedding. *Was he thinking about his own upcoming wedding?*

"Well, I think you should take my advice and maybe lower your weight count to five pounds. The heavier the weight you lift the larger the muscle mass you will add," he said.

"Lord knows I don't need to add anything," she replied, glancing over her shoulder to her ample bottom. She waited for him to make some type of flirtatious comment, but it never came. Suddenly, a voice came over the intercom paging him.

"That's me," he said, smiling again. "I hope to see you around here often Mrs…" he let the name trail off waiting for her to fill in the blank.

"It's Ms., but you can call me Pamela."

"Okay, Pamela. It was nice meeting you, but business calls," Sean replied before turning and walking away.

Terri walked back in her office a couple hours later, her legs and arms completely sore from her brief workout. Malik was on the phone with another possible prospect when he saw her come through the front door. She was wearing a pair of tight designer jeans, a yellow t-shirt that read *I Wanna Dance With Somebody*, and sneakers. Her hair was now in a ponytail held by one of those little spongy things. He wasn't used to seeing her in dress down mode, and it actually turned him on.

He watched her walk past his desk to her office and he hurried the caller along so that he could get the 411 on Mr. Sean Clemens. A few seconds later, Malik walked in Terris' office and saw her with her face buried in the crook of her arm down on her desk. He laughed as he walked up behind his boss and started to massage her shoulders. Something he'd done on numerous occasions.

"Mmmm." The light moan was innocent, but it shot straight to Malik's groin.

"You're getting old woman," he said playfully enjoying the scent of her Rhianna perfume and everything that was Terri mixing together.

"I'm not that damn old," she smiled as she grunted with pleasure from the feel of his large hands plying her sore muscles. "Ohhhh, yeah, right there," she said as Malik moved around her shoulder blades with professional strokes.

*Yeah, I can give it to you right here if you let me.* "How does that feel?" he asked, thankful she didn't know what he was thinking.

"I think you missed your calling," she replied softly.

Malik knew she was right, but not for the calling she was imagining. He missed the chance for his shot at being her man. That was the only calling he wanted to answer.

"How did it go with the Clemens?" Malik asked, his fingers kneading her lower back.

Terri eased her chair back, giving him more room to work. She knew this was inappropriate and was borderline sexual harassment, but damn did it feel good.

"I got a feeling you might be right about him," she mumbled against her arm. "But I'm going to give it one more shot before I involve Andre," she replied, hoping that Sean was only a cheater, and not a gay cheater.

"Suit yourself. You know I have never steered you wrong, and I never will." He let his hands glide up her sides slowly, letting his fingers graze the sides of her breast.

*Did he just touch my breast?* "I know Malik," she said softly. Her head eased to the side so he could work her neck. "How was your day without me?" she asked, drumming up more conversation. *My pussy is throbbing and I'm asking him about his damn day.*

Malik looked down and saw that his erection was very noticeable. *Damn.* He used one hand to shift his dick, but it only made it worse.

"It was slow up until a moment ago." *Slow. What a great word.* He trailed his fingers across the nape of her neck, enjoying the slight tremor he felt shudder through her.

"Mmm. Why, what happened?" The energy pulsing through her had her pressing her legs together adding pressure to her tingling clit.

Malik saw her leg action and closed his eyes tightly. He drew in a few deep breaths, trying to control his body. *If I don't stop touching her now I'm going to get fired, because im going to snatch her little ass up and flip her over this desk.*

Instantly, Malik pulled back and walked quickly over to the windows, making sure to keep his back to her. He cleared his throat and shook his head to clear it. "Check this out. You won't believe who called."

Terri felt lost and cold without his hands on her. She lifted her head from the desk and sat back in her chair watching him. Her body was relaxed in some places and throbbing in others. *Why did he stop?*

"You're going to have to just tell me. I'm too sore to be guessing," Terri replied, reaching up to where his hands were touching her neck only moments ago.

Malik looked over his shoulder at the smooth skin that she was rubbing on her neck and licked his lips. He coughed lightly to ease the tightening feeling in his throat.

"June Foster," he said, again facing the window.

"*The* June Foster that once ran for office?" she asked, all the while checking out his tight ass. *I'd like to squeeze that one day,* she thought smiling.

Malik turned slightly to catch a quick peek at her, then gave the outside view his attention once more. "Yup. She didn't give a reason for calling. She just left her number and asked that you call her back as soon as possible." *What is she smiling about?*

"Wow. I wonder what she wants." *I wonder if he can lift me. I always wanted to have sex like that.* She continued to stare at his back.

"You and me both," said Malik. Then his curiosity got the best of him and he turned to face her. He now had control of his body and was thankful that he wouldn't humiliate himself. "Terri?"

"Hmm?"

"What are you smiling about?"

A hot blush spread up her neck darkening her cheeks. Embarrassment was etched on her face and she snatched up the contents of the folder and began shuffling the papers.

"Nothing. I was um…only thinking about a few things I needed," she said, trying desperately not to look at him.

Malik could only hope that the one thing that she needed was him. Not wanting to make her feel uncomfortable any longer, he headed towards the door.

"That's all I have for now. I emailed you the number to reach June Foster."

"Okay," said Terri, still not looking up.

"Okay then," he said before leaving.

Terri dropped her head back on her arm and sighed. "Damn, he makes me so freaking hot," she whispered to the empty room.

# Chapter 4

Later that evening, Terri laid in her bed thinking about June Foster's call. She had been in the newspaper once or twice over the last year as she attempted to make a splash in the political world, but soon her upcoming campaign came to an end with no word as to why. Terri wondered what the unmarried socialite wanted with her company. Her curiosity is what drove her to return her call once Malik left her office. She didn't get an answer, so she left a message.

She was reaching for the remote to turn on the television to watch her favorite show, *The Preachers Of L.A*, when her cell started to vibrate. She looked at the call display and saw that it was Malik. Her belly got a warm feeling and she smiled, wondering what he wanted.

"You got to be crazy messing with my Detrick Haddin time," Terri said as a way of greeting.

Malik laughed. "You love that show, but refuse to step foot in a church," he replied still laughing.

She sucked her teeth, then laughed. "I go to church."

"Easter, Christmas, and New Years, does not

signify that you go to church. It means you're a visitor," he said laughing.

Terri laughed at his joke, warmed by the fact that they clicked so easily. "Whatever sinner. What's up?"

"I'll tell you what's up. I just heard from Andre and he wants' to meet with you tonight. You're not going to believe what he has to say. I told him we could all meet at that little jazz spot you like in about an hour."

"I guess duty calls. Give me a second to get ready. Oh Malik, would you mind picking me up? I really don't feel like driving," Terri said blocking a yawn with her hand.

"Sure thing. I'll see you in an hour," he said, pleased that she'd asked.

As soon as the call ended, Terri jumped up off her bed and headed for the closet in search of something to wear. It had been several months since she had been to Rachael's Jazz Club, but it was one of her favorite spots. The last time she was there she had the pleasure of meeting Morgan Freeman who was in town filming some new movie about a serial killer. Najee had been on stage playing then, and the atmosphere was laid back and relaxing, just the way she liked it.

She riffled through the dresses in her closet and chose an all black fitted Faryn number that she had ordered from Lafayette 148 of New York. It was the proper attire to get away with a pair of comfortable Channel Sandals.

Terri showered, dressed, and bumped her hair a

little before spraying on a little Rhianna. She looked at her watch as her phone vibrated again and she smiled. It was exactly one hour later and she didn't have to be a genius to know that it would be Malik calling to let her know he was downstairs. Malik may have been late for a lot of things, but never for a night out on the town.

She was lucky that the elevator was already on her floor and she was downstairs in a matter of minutes. Making her way over to his car, she wasn't aware that his eyes followed the sway of her hips with every step. Terri got into Malik's car and he drove off heading to Rachael's. She noticed that Malik was wearing a cologne that smelled really good, and she inhaled deeply enjoying the play it had on her hormones.

She turned her head slightly noticing how very distinguished he looked in his black shirt and slacks. His clothes looked a lot more expensive than what he usually would wear to work, and she found him sexy and appealing. Her eyes roamed down his chest to settle at his crotch and she sucked in her bottom lip when she noticed the outline of his dick. *Damn.* Shaking her head, Terri decided to spark up a conversation to get her mind off the way her employee filled out his pants.

"Hey, I tried to contact that lady, but she didn't answer," she said glancing out the window.

"You're talking about that Foster woman?" he asked, glancing at her briefly before turning his attention back to the road. "That lady is a trip. I wondered what made her run for office. When I looked her up, she didn't seem to have any qualifications that would make her a good candidate to get elected. The funny thing I noticed is that she has a law degree, but she doesn't practice. She didn't even want to go into detail with me about what she needed Vows for. In fact, she was adamant about only speaking to you."

"Well, I did my part, so we shall see," she said as they pulled up to the jazz club.

Malik parked and got out to open Terri's door. Her long, sleek legs swung out as her Channel sandals met the concrete. He sighed under his breath as he glimpsed at how smooth her skin was. *I would love to trail my hands up those long ass legs starting from her pretty petite feet.*

Terri took Maliks' hand and together they entered the club. She could feel his hand resting on her back as he guided her through the crowd to the back of the establishment. When she had to stop suddenly because some guy wanted to pass by, he was caught off guard and he pressed into her from behind. There was no mistaken the firm bulge she felt against her behind and it sent a fireball straight between her thighs.

"Excuse me," Malik whispered near her ear as they continued to move on.

His warm, minty breath fanning out over her face didn't help the situation. "Mmm," was all she could manage to say.

Inside, Andre Harper sat in a corner booth

drinking something that was blue and filled with all sorts of fruit. He waved over his boss and co-worker when he saw them enter the club. Andre smiled as he watched them making their way over to his table. *They look good together*, he thought to himself. Once they were at his table, he stood and shook hands with Malik, and planted a friendly kiss on the side of Terri's face.

"So the company has a new interest I see," he said, smiling as they all sat back down.

The waitress came to the table, and Malik ordered himself a Hennessy, and Terri a glass of Pinot. She was impressed again that Malik remembered what she liked. They hadn't been out together since last years company Christmas party. She smiled, remembering how attentive he had been. *He's so nice to me. Hmm.*

"Yes, Sean Clemens. And Malik says that you have some pertinent information about this prospect," Terri said, wanting to get all the information she could on the client.

Andre Harper smiled before taking the straw in his mouth. He took a sip of his drink and sighed in pleasure.

"Let's just say that I'm a member of an elite society that he is also a member of. Actually, tomorrow he and I are supposed to meet on the second level of his establishment," said Andre, offering his little tidbit of information.

"You mean his gym?" asked Malik.

"Yup."

"And what about this elite society?" Terri questioned.

"Boss, excuse me if I seem impartial, but I cannot break my oath to the society and reveal too much information. It would be against our code of ethic's. But, what I can tell you is that Malik's assessment is on point."

"I need some proof Andre," Terri said as she toyed with a napkin.

The sound of music playing came from the stage as the piano player started to play a familiar melody. A second later, Terri noticed the long curly head gentlemen emerge from behind a curtain playing a saxophone. It was *Kenny G*. He blended in with the piano as they mimicked his version of *Songbird*.

"I can get myself in a lot of trouble Terri, but you know how I love to live on the edge. And on top of that I love my job. It pays well. I'm going to go above the call of duty on this one," said Andre smiling. "You'll have your proof tomorrow," said Andre, standing up.

"Thank you, Andre," said Terri, looking up at him. "And remember our policy."

"I know, I know. I can push it to the limit, but no sexual intercourse," he said with a sexy smile on his face. "Damn shame though," he said, shaking his head pouting. Then instantly, he perked back up. "Well, I have to be going now. I'm sure the company can pick up the check," he said with a giggle before he turned to leave.

Malik lifted his glass and took a swallow of his

drink. "Now that we got that cleared up, hopefully this case will be a piece of cake," he said, placing the glass back on the dark wooden table.

"It's a damn shame, all these down low brother's out here," said Terri frowning. "I just can't stand a man that would lead a woman to believe that she's his prize, and behind closed doors, she's not even the wrapping paper covering the gift."

"You know I feel you on that," Malik said, toying with his glass. He started to raise the glass to his lips, but changed his mind. "Enough of this work business. Now that we're out, let's see if the boss remembers how to dance."

He stood up and extended his hand for Terri to grab. Terri was on her second glass of wine and feeling tipsy, and she was definitely in the mood for a dance. She accepted Maliks' hand, and he guided her out to the center of Rachael's dance floor.

When she laid her head on his shoulders, she realized just how long it had been since she was in the comforts of a man's embrace. Malik's arms felt strong and safe around her, and she snuggled closer. The smell of his cologne began to work on her hormones once again and she welcomed the throbbing that began between her thighs.

Malik was trying everything in his power to keep his body under control, but the feel of Terri pressed intimately against him had his lower region rising to the occasion. *Smart idea, idiot*, he berated himself. He felt like a randy kid on his first date with the girl he's always wanted. He looked down at her and felt his chest tighten with an emotion he wasn't yet ready to label.

Throughout the night they drank, laughed, and danced the night away in each others arms having no care for the outside world around them. Nothing could have prepared either of them for the plateau of emotions that filled up within them, eager to burst free.

The alcohol moving through Terri's system had long since put her good judgement and common sense to bed. Right now, she was operating on pure lustful instinct. Her mind was telling her to slow down, but her body was chanting go for it.

She felt his dick pressed into her stomach and eased a little closer. *Mmm, Malik is packing*, she thought as she dipped against him enjoying the bulge that was so evident between them. Malik flexed his hips against her and she heard him groan in pleasure. *Oh, he likes that, huh? Time to be brave Terri.*

"Do you want to get out of here?" she whispered close to his ear, her arms draped around his neck as they swayed to the music. They were pressed together breast to chest and hips to thigh, and she eagerly tightened her hold on him. She could feel her breast get heavy, and the lace of her bra made her nipples sensitive.

Malik could see that Terri was two shades to the wind, and he figured it was the reason why she was touching and grinding on him on the dance floor. He wouldn't let her get too out of hand, and he damn sure wasn't going to let her dance with anyone else. *Fuck that.*

He looked down at her drunken grin and smiled. "I was just about to ask the same thing," Malik said as he began escorting her off the dance floor and toward the front door. It was time to get little Ms. Drunken Monkey into bed.

## Chapter 5

Terri woke up next to Malik in his Westside condo with a groggy head. Her mouth was dry and felt like cotton. Her eyes were gritty and she had to blink several times to clear her vision. She had no idea what came over her last night, and no idea what happened. She couldn't remember a damn thing and she just hoped she hadn't done anything stupid.

Glancing over at Malik, she saw that he was still sleeping. He wasn't wearing a shirt and she dreaded the fact that they might have slept together. Even though it was something that she'd daydreamed about, she didn't want it to happen like this.

Terri lifted the sheet they were under and released a sigh of relief when she saw that she was still fully dressed, and he still wore his pants. *He had been a gentleman,* she thought smiling. Any other guy probably would have taken advantage of her.

Knowing she had to get up and start her day, she planted a kiss on his cheek taking care not to wake him. She grabbed her purse and tiptoed out the room. Once in the living room, she used her cell phone to call a cab.

Having only ten minutes before the cab would get

there, Terri went back inside the bedroom to find her shoes. She saw them on the floor near the bed and quietly made her way over. She looked down at Malik lying there with the black silk sheet covering his lower body. She never knew that he had several tattoo's and made a mental note to ask him about them. She picked up her shoes, and glanced over her shoulder one last time before leaving. *I wonder what making love to him would be like?*

\*\*\*\*

Terri had just stepped from the building when her cab pulled up. She hopped in the back seat ready to get her day on its way.

"Where to Miss?"

"Twenty third and Pavilion," she said, leaning back in the seat. This cabby must really love his job, because his cab looked immaculate. Not a speck of dirt anywhere, and it smelled like spring flowers.

The driver pulled up to Twenty third in record time. "Here we are Miss."

"Would you be able to wait? I just need to run into the cleaner's real fast," she said, her hand resting on the door handle.

"Sure, I'll wait."

Terri smiled in gratitude. "Thanks. I'll only be a minute or two."

She slid from the cab, and hurried inside Chu's Cleaners. The only thing on her mind was grabbing the outfits that had been sitting there for almost two months. *I hope they haven't sold my shit.*

On her way out the cleaners with her clothing she

was happy to see that the cab driver had waited as promised. Before she could open the door to get back in the cab, a strange woman bumped into her. Terri quickly checked her pocket for her Coach wallet, knowing that she wasn't actually in the best area of town.

"No need to check for your money Ms. Powell," the stranger said.

"Excuse me, do I know you? How do you know my name?" Terri asked confused. Although the woman looked familiar, she still wasn't about to let down her guard.

She hoped Malik didn't have a deranged girlfriend that had followed her and was now ready to cut her from ear to ear. She hadn't had a fight since high school, and even back then, she had lost. Today would probably be no different.

The strange woman gave the cab driver a signal, and he pulled off leaving Terri standing there with an arm full of clothes, and no way to get home.

The woman pointed to a little shabby coffee shop on the corner across the street. "Do you mind if we go over and have a cup of coffee?"

"I'm not going anywhere with you until you tell me who you are," Terri insisted.

"You honestly don't know who I am?" the woman asked, as if everyone in the world should know who she was. She figured she should be recognized from all the times her picture had been in magazines and newspapers.

"If I knew, I wouldn't have asked you," said Terri,

becoming bored with the *guess who* game.

"I'm June. June Foster. I got your message last night, but I didn't want to really meet at your office," June explained.

Recognition replaced the irritation on Terri's face after finding out who the woman was. She felt a little foolish knowing she had been looking at photos of her only hours ago, and had already forgotten how she looked. *That's because you were totally distracted by Malik and wondering if he could lift your nasty ass.*

Terri looked the woman up and down, the same way she had done to her. She noticed the designer clothing and shoes, and the expensive jewelry draped around her neck, and almost laughed at how out of place she looked. It actually made sense that she would look out of place, especially with her sister Ivy Wallace owning one of the hottest makeup and natural hair products on the market today called Shades of Ivy. Terri actually uses some of the Shades of Ivy products on occasion and she knew exactly what the family was worth.

Terri rearranged the clothes she was carrying, switching them to her other arm, and figured that it couldn't do much harm to accompany the lady to the coffee shop. Besides her ride was probably half way across town now since she'd sent him on his way.

\*\*\*\*

Ralph's Coffee House was a quiet place that looked like it catered more to the homeless and people of the nightlife who were trying to get a cup of cheap dark medicine to wake them up before returning to work. There was a fat burly guy behind a smeared stainless steel counter making breakfast croissant's and a little old pale faced lady taking orders. Her outfit resembled something from the television show *Mel's Diner*, and looked as though it hadn't been washed since the network cut the sitcom.

June sized the woman up sitting across from her feeling a little uncomfortable and threatened by Terri's flawless beauty. Even with her hair a little messed up she was still stunning. She had followed Terri and Malik last night, and staked out Malik's building all night. She knew that her hair was only out of place right now because she must have indulged in some extra curricular activities with her employee, which was none of her business. She was here for her own reasons. Nothing else.

"So your company sort of portrays you to be like Will Smith in that movie Hitch. Is that true?" June asked, successfully hiding her sarcasm.

"My God, no," Terri replied. "We're actually the opposite of that. I'm not hired to get two people together. I get hired to see if they can actually stay together."

"You mean you aim to break them up?" June questioned with hope.

Terri shook her head. "No. Not at all. Vows is a company set up to see if a person's faithfulness will endure. Where called if someone has any doubt that their significant other is cheating and wishes to find out," said Terri, answering the woman's question without pause.

At that moment the old waitress came over and sat two cups of coffee down in front of each of them. Terri looked down into her cup refusing to drink out of the hideously dirty cup. There was actually a smudge of lipstick on the side of the cup. She frowned down into the dark, murky liquid and picked up her spoon planning to stir the coffee around until she left.

The questions that June was asking had been asked hundreds of times by other clients, and she was always prepared with an answer. Terri listened to June go into detail about what she wanted to use Vows services for. She listened with a trained ear and felt a little doubtful.

Since she wasn't in her office where she'd usually conduct these kind of meetings, she decided to take precautions for legal matters. She pretended to check her phone for missed calls while June was still giving her details on why she needed her services. She slid her phone in her lap and pressed the button to record their conversation discreetly.

"I know that I didn't leave any details with your assistant, but I'm actually here on behalf of my sister. She's very successful, and it's my job to make sure she is safe, and doesn't get deceived or conned by anyone."

"You mean Ivy Wallace?" Terri asked, even though she already knew who she was referring to. She took a small tube of lipstick out of her purse and placed it on the table in front of June. "This Ivy Wallace, correct?"

A brief shutter of annoyance crossed June's face when she looked down at Ivy's brand of lipstick, but she concealed it well. "Yes, that Ivy Wallace," she said with a slight rudeness to her tone, but quickly hid it behind a fake cough. She plastered a smile on her face that almost seemed painful.

"She is indeed my baby sister, and very very rich. She has her own organic hair products called *'Naturally You'*, a new makeup line called *'Shades of Ivy'*, and she just released her perfume line called *'I: The Frangrance of Me'*. That's why I have to be as discreet about this as possible. I don't want her involved in any scandals."

"Okay. So what exactly do you want from me?" asked Terri, placing the lipstick back in her bag.

"I need to hire you because of her husband, Nathaniel. I know Nate is a scum bag, but Ivy refuses to see it. I need proof."

Terri sat up straighter in her seat. "Let me get this straight. You want me to check things out on your sister's husband?" When June nodded, Terri went on. "I just seen an article saying that she and her husband Nathaniel Wallace, just returned from a lavish vacation in Aspen, where they renewed their vows," said Terri frowning in confusion.

"Don't believe everything you see in the tabloids Ms. Powell. I'm pretty sure that you're a much more informed woman than that paper trash you find in the Publix checkout lines," said June. "Nate is a failing pig whose law firm is nothing more than a cover up for how broke he really is. It was Nate who ruined my chances at making it into political office, but there's no need to go into that," she said feeling her temper getting the best of her.

*Hmm, someone is a little bitter*, thought Terri.

"After backing out of the politicians running, my sister gave me a position at her company as head of procurement, and I have no complaints about that," said June. She saw the look on Terri's face and didn't want her to think she was doing this out of jealousy.

"I just know that Ivy has always had a hard time picking the right man, and it worries me. This is where your company comes in. I want you to find out what you can and do whatever's necessary so that I can be sure my sister hasn't made another mistake. Just name your fee and the money will be wired to your account by noon," she said looking anxious.

Terri was not going to pass up the chance to take on this case. She didn't know exactly how much of the story June was telling was accurate, but it was a chance to take Vows up a notch and gain new clients.

"Okay, June. Text me a fax number where I can send our contract, and I would be happy to have my assistant prepare it and send it over to you."

"That would be that Malik fellow that lives in that building you slept at last night?" When Terri's mouth dropped open, she quickly rushed on. "Look, no contracts. Just tell me the amount you need to handle the case, and I will wire the money to your account. It's that simple," she said sarcastically.

Terri had wanted to snap on June for her rude remark about where she'd slept, but she had gotten cut off before she could reply. But, June's next statement had Terri noticing how the woman was getting weirder by the minute. It was all a little too secretive for her. Looking for a little revenge for the smart ass comment about Malik, she decided to tripple her normal fee expecting June to pitch a bitch about it, but that didn't happen.

"Agreed. I'll wire one hundred and fifty thousand to your account by noon," she said before standing and tossing a twenty dollar bill on the table. She walked out without saying another word, not even caring that Terri didn't have a ride home.

Terri lifted her cell from her lap and stopped the recording. She didn't know what was going on, but it wasn't her job to investigate the family secrets of her clients. Her job was to tempt the selected spouse and see if they would stay faithful. Period. Whatever else was going on in the Foster and Wallace family was none of her business.

Terri called another cab, and after receiving confirmation that it was on its way, she called Malik. She wanted to tell him about what just transpired, but his voice mail picked up, so she figured she would catch him at the office later on today.

Grabbing up her clothing items, she decided to wait outside, and left the café. She stood in the early morning sunshine thinking about Malik and everything that happened last night. She felt little butterflies in her stomach, along with a now familiar ache between her thighs whenever he crossed her mind. She didn't have any idea that Malik could be so much fun. She smiled, wondering what he was doing right at this minute.

Her eyes were gritty and she had to blink several times to clear her vision. She had no idea what came over her last night, and no idea what happened. She couldn't remember a damn thing and she just hoped she hadn't done anything stupid.

Glancing over at Malik, she saw that he was still sleeping. He wasn't wearing a shirt and she dreaded the fact that they might have slept together. Even though it was something that she'd daydreamed about, she didn't want it to happen like this.

Terri lifted the sheet they were under and released a sigh of relief when she saw that she was still fully dressed, and he still wore his pants. *He had been a gentleman,* she thought smiling. Any other guy probably would have taken advantage of her.

Knowing she had to get up and start her day, she planted a kiss on his cheek taking care not to wake him. She grabbed her purse and tiptoed out the room. Once in the living room, she used her cell phone to call a cab.

Having only ten minutes before the cab would get there, Terri went back inside the bedroom to find her shoes. She saw them on the floor near the bed and quietly made her way over. She looked down at

Malik lying there with the black silk sheet covering his lower body. She never knew that he had several tattoo's and made a mental note to ask him about them. She picked up her shoes, and glanced over her should one last time before leaving. *I wonder what making love to him would be like?*

Terri had just stepped from the building when her cab pulled up. She hopped in the back seat and ready to get her day on the way.

"Where to Miss?"

"Twenty third and Pavilion," she said, leaning back in the seat. This cabby must really love his job because his cab looked immaculate. Not a speck of dirt anywhere, and it smelled like spring flowers.

The driver pulled up to Twenty third in record time. "Here we are Miss."

"Would you be able to wait? I just need to run into the cleaner's real fast," she said, her hand resting on the door handle.

"Sure, Miss. I'll wait."

Terri smiled in gratitude. "Thanks. I'll only be a minute or two."

She slid from the cab, and hurried inside Chu's Cleaners, the only thing on her mind was grabbing the outfits that had been sitting there for almost two months. *I hope they haven't sold my shit.*

On her way out the cleaners with her clothing she was happy to see that the cab driver had waited as promised. Before she could open the door to get back in the cab, a strange woman bumped into her. Terri quickly checked her pocket for her Coach wallet, knowing that she wasn't actually in the best area of town.

"No need to check for your money Ms. Powell," the stranger said.

"Excuse me, do I know you? How do you know my name?" Terri asked confused. Although the woman looked familiar, she still wasn't about to let down her guard.

She hoped Malik didn't have a deranged girlfriend that had followed her and was now ready to cut her from ear to ear. She hadn't had a fight since high school, and even back then, she had lost. Today would probably be no different.

The strange woman gave the cab driver a signal, and he pulled off, leaving Terri standing there with an arm full of clothes, and no way to get home.

The woman pointed to a little shabby coffee shop on the corner across the street. "Do you mind if we go over and have a cup of coffee?"

"I'm not going anywhere with you until you tell me who you are," Terri insisted.

"You honestly don't know who I am?" she asked, as if the world should know who she was. She figured she should be recognized from all the times her picture was in magazines and newspapers.

"If I knew, I wouldn't have asked you," said Terri, becoming bored with the *guess who* game.

"I'm June. June Foster. I got your message last night, but I didn't want to really meet at your office," June explained.

Suddenly, Terri knew exactly who the woman

was. She felt a little foolish knowing she had been looking at photos of her only hours ago, and had already forgotten how she looked. *That's because you were totally distracted by Malik and wondering if he could lift your nasty ass.*

Terri looked the woman up and down, the same way she had done to her. She noticed the designer clothing, shoes, and expensive jewelry draped around her neck and almost laughed at how out of place she looked. It actually made sense that she would look out of place, especially with her sister owning one of the hottest makeup and natural hair products on the market today called Shades of Ivy. Terri had actually used some of her products on occasion and she knew exactly what the family was worth.

Terri rearranged the clothes she was carrying, switching them to her other arm, and figured that it couldn't do much harm to accompany the lady to the coffee shop. Besides her ride was probably half way across town now since she'd sent him on his way.

****

Ralph's Coffee House was a quiet place that looked like it catered more to the homeless and people of the nightlife who were trying to get a cup of cheap dark medicine to wake them up before returning to work. There was a fat burly guy behind a foggy stainless steel counter making breakfast croissant's and a little old white lady taking orders. Her outfit resembled something from the television show *Mel's Diner*, and looked as though it hadn't been washed since the network cut the sitcom.

June sized the woman up sitting across from her feeling a little uncomfortable and threatened by Terri's flawless beauty. Even with her hair a little messed up she was stunning. She had followed Terri and Malik last night, and staked out Malik's building. She knew that her hair was only out of place right now because she must have indulged in some extra curricular activities with her employee, which was none of her business. She was here on business. Nothing else.

"So your company sort of portrays you to be like Will Smith in that movie Hitch, huh?" June asked, successfully hiding her sarcasm.

"My God, no," Terri replied. "We're actually the opposite of that. I'm not hired to get two people together. I get hired to see if they can actually stay together."

"You mean you aim to break them up?" June questioned with hope.

Terri shook her head. "No. Not at all. Vow's is a company set up to see if one's faithfulness will endure until the end. That is if one has any doubt in mind that their significant other is cheating," said Terri answering the woman's question without pause.

At that moment the old waitress came over and sat two cups of coffee down in front of each of them. Terri looked down into her cup refusing to drink out of the hideous dirty cup. She picked up her spoon planning to stir the liquid around until she left.

The questions that June was asking had been asked hundreds of times by other clients, and she was always prepared with an answer. Terri listened to June go into detail about what she wanted to use Vow's services for. She listened with a trained ear and felt a little doubtful.

Since she wasn't in her office where she'd usually conduct these kind of meetings, she decided to take precautions for legal matters. She pretended to check her phone for missed calls while June was still giving her details on why she needed her services. She slid her phone in her lap and pressed the button to record their conversation discreetly.

"I know that I didn't leave any details with your assistant, but I'm actually here on behalf of my sister. She's very successful, and it's my job to make sure she is safe, and doesn't get deceived or conned by anyone."

"You mean Ivy Wallace?" Terri asked, even though she already knew who she was referring to. She took a small tube of lipstick out of her purse and placed it on the table in front of June. "This Ivy Wallace, correct?"

A brief shutter of annoyance crossed June's face, but she concealed it well. "Yes, that Ivy Wallace," she said with a slight rudeness to her tone, but quickly hid it behind a fake cough. She plastered a smile on her face that almost seemed painful.

"She is indeed my baby sister, and very very rich.

She has her own organic hair products called '*Naturally You*', a new makeup line called '*Shades of Ivy*', and she just released her perfume line called '*I: The Frangrance of Me*', which allows you to have your very own scent created. That's why I have to be as discreet about this as possible. I don't want her caught up in any scandals."

"And what exactly do you want from me?" asked Terri.

"I need to hire you because of her husband, Nathaniel. I know Nate is a scum bag, but Ivy refuses to see it. I need proof."

Terri sat up straighter in her seat. "Let me get this straight. You want me to check things out on your sister's husband?" When June nodded, Terri went on. "I just seen an article saying that she and her husband Nathaniel Wallace, just returned from a lavish vacation in Aspen, where they renewed their vows," said Terri frowning in confusion.

"Don't believe everything you see in the tabloids Ms. Powell. I'm pretty sure that you're a much more informed woman than that paper trash you find in the Publix checkout lines," said June. "Nate is a failing pig whose law firm is nothing more than a cover up for how broke he really is. It was Nate who ruined my chances at making it into political office, but there's no need to go into that," she said feeling her temper getting the best of her.

"My sister has given me a position at her company as head of procurement and I have no complaints about that. I just know that she has always had a hard time picking the right man, and it worries me. This is where your company comes in. I want you to find out what you can and do whatever's necessary so that I can be sure my sister hasn't made another mistake. Just name your fee and the money will be wired to your account by noon," she said looking anxious.

Terri was not going to pass up the chance to take on this case. She didn't know exactly how much of the story June was telling was accurate, but it was a chance to take Vow's to the next level and gain new clients.

"Okay, June. Text me a fax number where I can send our contract, and I would be happy to have my assistant prepare it, and send it over to you."

"That would be that Malik fellow that lives in that building you slept at last night?" When Terri's mouth dropped open, she quickly rushed on. "Look no contracts. Just tell me the amount you need to handle the case, and I will wire the money to your account. It's that simple," she said sarcastically.

Terri had wanted to slap June for her rude remark about where she'd slept, but she had gotten cut off before she could reply. But, June's next statement had Terri noticing how the woman was getting weirder by the minute. Looking for a little revenge for the smart ass comment about Malik, she decided to tripple her normal fee expecting June to pitch a bitch about it, but that didn't happen.

"Agreed. I'll wire one hundred thousand to your account by noon," she said before standing and tossing a twenty dollar bill on the table. She walked out without saying another word, not even caring that Terri didn't have a ride home.

Terri lifted her cell from her lap and stopped the recording. She didn't know what was going on, but it wasn't her job to investigate the family secrets of her clients. Her job was to tempt the selected spouse and see if they would stay faithful. Period. Whatever else was going on in the Foster and Wallace family was none of her business.

Terri called another cab, and after receiving confirmation that it was on its way, she called Malik. She wanted to tell him about what just transpired, but his voice mail picked up, so she figured she would catch him at the office later on today.

Grabbing up her clothing items, she decided to wait outside, and left the café. She stood in the early morning sunshine thinking about Malik and everything that happened last night. She felt little butterflies in her stomach, along with a now familiar ache between her thighs whenever he crossed her mind. She didn't have any idea that Malik could be so much fun. She smiled, wondering what he was doing right at this minute.

## Chapter 6
### Two Days Later...

The smell of blueberry muffins was wafting through the air of the tiny bakery that sat nestled in the center of the downtown shopping district. The place was small and people stood outside or sat in the few chairs placed around the metal tables, waiting their chance to get inside and place an order.

Terri had stood in that very line for almost fifteen minutes to finally get inside and purchase a half dozen oatmeal raisin cookies. Her ultimate weakness. There was nothing on earth that could make her part with one.

She smiled, remembering when she and Malik had gotten into an argument over the cookies. She had been down to her last one, and was saving it for a late night binge while sitting in front of the television. But Malik had other plans.

He came by one night with important paperwork she'd forgotten at work. While she was in the bathroom, she made the mistake of telling him to make himself at home and help himself to whatever was in the kitchen. When she joined him in the kitchen, it was just in time to see him pop the last bite of the cookie into his mouth. That was the one and only time she had raised her voice at him.

The feel of her cell phone vibrating on the table while in her purse brought her back to the present. She pulled the phone out and swiped the key to answer the call.

"Terry Powell."

"Ms. Powell, this is June Foster. I have an extra ticket to a charity ball for tonight and I want you to go. It will be the perfect opportunity for you to get a close look at Nathaniel, and perhaps even make your first attempt at him."

Terri was taken by surprise by the woman's forward attitude. "Tonight is short notice Ms. Foster. For something like this I'd need time to prepare."

June scoffed at her attempt at getting out of the invitation. "Nonsense, Ms. Powell. I know this isn't the first time you've been to a charity event, and I'm sure you have something nice enough to wear. I'll have the invitation delivered to your office. See you tonight."

Eyes wide, Terri stared down at the phone in her hand. "What the hell!"

Feeling like she had just been railroaded, Terri stood up with her cookie purchase, and left. She was fuming as she made her way to her car, thinking the whole walk over, that June was too damn bossy.

"Once I get to the charity event tonight I'm going to pull her ass aside and give her a piece of my mind."

With that being said, she was still beholding to their agreement to pursue Nathaniel. She sighed loudly and kept walking. Instead of going to her car, she made a detour and stepped inside a Gucci Boutique. The sales lady was a rail thin blonde rocking a white Merlin Jade halter jumper. The fabric was a thin cotton and was perfect for the L. A. heat. Her heels were four inches and complimented the outfit flawlessly. When the woman saw Terri step inside, she perked up and headed her way.

"Hi," she said, showing all her ultra bright white teeth. "I'm Cathy. You look like a woman that needs something right away," she said with a light laugh.

Terri instantly warmed up to the woman's friendly demeanor. "Yes, I need an evening gown for a charity event tonight. But, let me warn you, I'm a little picky. It takes me hours to choose a pair of shoes," she said smiling.

Cathy laughed and tucked her arm through Terri's. "Don't worry. I already know exactly what you need." She pulled Terri into a small private dressing room offering her a seat in one of the cream Tess Wingback chairs. "Would you like some tea, coffee, or water?"

"No thank you."

"Very well then. I'll return in a moment. I have the perfect dress for you."

Cathy hurried down a hallway and disappeared through a door marked private. While she was gone, Terri checked her phone for messages. She was sorting through her emails when the woman returned carrying a garment bag and a white shoe box. She hung the hanger of the garment bag on a silver hook and placed the box on the table.

"Here we are," she said, unzipping the bag carefully.

Terri sat back watching, waiting for Cathy to present this *'perfect'* dress. When the material was pulled free of the nylon bag, a slow smile transformed Terri's face. *Hot damn that dress was hot!*

"Wow," was the only word Terri was able to speak.

"I know right," Cathy murmured while gazing at the dress.

It's glamorous white chiffon sweetheart flowers delicately covered the bodice, tapering at the waistline accented with tiny white pearls. The bottom of the dress formed a short drape before the skirt continued in a silken fall trailing out behind.

Terri stood up and touched the silk and smiled at how light the material felt.

"It's your size. And so are the shoes," said Cathy softly, not wanting to interrupt the way the dress was hypnotizing her customer.

Terri glanced at Cathy, a confused frown on her face. "How do you know my dress and shoe size? I've never shopped here before."

"Because it's my job and I'm almost always right." She opened the white box, revealing a pair of silver high heel Gucci sandals. "Is this your size?"

Terri peer down into the box and nodded her head in amazement. She then peeked at the size of the dress and broke out into a wide smile. "Damn, you're good."

"Thank you," Cathy said, beaming with pride. "So, do you like this or would you like to see something else?"

"Oh, no. This is perfect. It's exactly what I need. I'll take it."

She reached into her purse and handed her a black credit card. After viewing the dress she now felt a little excited about the charity event. Terri signed the receipt, thanked the sales clerk, and started back in the direction of her car.

"I might not want to be at the event, but I might as well look good while I'm there," she said with some added pep in her step.

When she got to her car she opened the back door and hooked the garment bag on one of the hooks near the door to keep it from getting damaged. After securing the gown, she slid behind the wheel and reached for her purse. She pulled out her phone and dialed the office.

"Vows, this is Malik speaking. How can I help you?"

Terri grinned like a teenager at the sound of his voice over the phone. Even though he sounded all business like, his voice was still able to send a warm sensation down between her thighs.

"I don't know. What can you do?"

Malik chuckled into the receiver. "You better stop flirting with me before I take you up on your offer."

At a lost for words, she sat there looking down at

his image on her screen.

"Yeah, that's what I thought," he said laughing. "Where are you? I thought you would be in by now."

Terri cleared her throat, trying to regain her composure. His threat had shaken her up, but in a good way. "Umm, I umm…"

"Take your time." Malik closed his eyes, trying to picture how she looked right now, all frustrated and confused.

"I'm not coming in today," she blurted out. *Why do I feel like he's the boss and im calling out?*

That got Malik's attention. He opened his eyes and sat up straight in his chair.

"What do you mean you're not coming in? Is something wrong?"

Terri never took off from work unless she was too sick to make it in. Just last year she tried coming in when she had the flu, and Malik had to threaten to tie her to the bed if she did.

"No, nothing's wrong. I got invited to a charity ball at the last minute, and I need to get myself together."

"Oh."

The flat 'oh' was all that he said, and Terri sat on the phone waiting for him to say something else, but he didn't. It made her feel guilty, so she started explaining about who had invited her.

"I was at the bakery this morning when I got a call from June. She sort of insisted that I show up to the ball. She thought it would be a good chance for me to get a line on Nathaniel. You know, see how he moves and whatnot."

Malik didn't say anything. He'd heard about the ball last week. It had been on the front page of the society section in the newspaper. He wasn't upset that Terri was going to the ball. It was work. He understood that. *Then why are you sitting here like an ass making her feel uncomfortable?*, he asked himself.

That's easy to answer. He was jealous. Plain and simple. He knew she would eventually be asked to dance, and he envisioned all the men there vying for her attention. Malik bit down hard, grinding his teeth in frustration. *I know how to stop that shit from happening.*

"Did you need me to go with you as an escort. I already have a tux. There's no need for you to go alone." *Say yes, say yes*, he chanted to himself.

"No, that won't be necessary," she said not wanting to force him to go. "You can stay there and hold down the fort while I take care of this. I don't intend to stay long anyway. I'll scope out the subject while rubbing elbows with the rich folks. This will be nothing more than a way to pull in more clients while sipping some very expensive champagne while sporting my new dress."

Malik frowned. "You bought a new dress? Sounds like you're trying to make an impression on some of the men that will be there," he said with a strained laugh.

Terri heard the sarcasm in his tone and tensed up. "I didn't know I had to have your permission to spend my money. And if I wanted to make an impression, I damn well can," she snapped.

*Damn, I've pissed her off.* "I'm sorry Terri. I didn't mean it like that. I'm being an asshole."

"You don't own me Malik. I don't belong to you."

Her words packed a punch, and Malik drew back, securely put in his place. *You don't belong to me yet.* "You're right, and I apologize for the remark. I had no right to say that to you. I just…"

Terri took a deep breath to calm herself down. His apology was sincere and she didn't want to be mad at him. "You just what?"

Malik drew in a deep breath and decided to be honest with her. To put his cards on the table and see what happened. If she shot him down, then he'd know that his feeling were one sided, and he'd step back.

"I don't want you falling for someone else. You know. Some rich guy might come and sweep you off your feet or something. I don't think I could handle that."

A slow smile eased across Terri's lips. "Why do you care?"

*Okay, here goes nothing.* "Because, if anyone's going to sweep you off your feet, it's going to be me." *There. I said it.*

Terri was sporting a full fledge toothy grin now. She was sitting in her car cheesing it up while people were walking pass, not paying her any attention.

*He wants to sweep me off my feet,* she said to herself. A little giggle slipped out, and she slapped her hand over her mouth quickly.

"Terri?"

"Oh, um. Wow, look at the time. I have to get going. I'll call you as soon as I get in. Bye."

She pressed the button to end the call and stared down at his smiling face on her cell phone screen.

"Yesssss! Yes! Yes! Yes." She pumped her fist in the air and whooped and hollered. Several people glanced in her car's direction before they continued on their way.

"Now what?" she said out loud.

*Now, I'll go to this ball, and then…we'll see.*

\*\*\*\*

Hours later, Malik sat at his desk thinking about Terri. He sighed heavily leaning back in his seat. She was never too far from his thoughts and that was fine by him. He wondered what she thought about what he'd said to her today about wanting to sweep her off her feet. She had ended the call abruptly after that. *Maybe I finally got to her. Or maybe she doesn't feel the same. Damn, did I move too fast?*

Although the two of them had been having dinner several nights, it didn't mean they were dating. It was always work involved. But that night when they had left Rachael's Jazz club together, he thought for sure that he was going to see his fantasy come to life.

Malik couldn't remember the last time he'd been so ready. Terri wasn't like any of the women that he would find himself waking up to on his weekend rendezvous. His interest in her was more than just some night club conquest that came a dime a dozen. No his interest was much more than just sex.

The ringing of the phone jogged him from his thoughts.

"Vows, how may I help you?"

"If you looked at the caller ID display sometime's you would see who this is," the familiar voice said.

"Oh, hey Andre. Did you get everything we needed?" asked Malik.

"You bet I did. Hell, that was the best assignment a guy could have," he said laughing.

His night with Sean Clemens had been hot. He just wished he could have gone all the way with him and slammed his dick in his tight little ass. But Vows had a no sex rule, and he wasn't going to break it. Shit, he loved his job, and the pay was awesome.

Andre Harper was a good looking man. His thick wavy hair and smoldering dark eyes weren't only attractive to women, but also to some of the Bay's most prominent men. For years he'd pushed away beautiful women that tried to give him action because they weren't what he wanted. When he decided to 'come out' five years ago, after being sick of the closet life, he felt like a brand new human being. His sexuality was something that he was proud of despite those that felt differently.

Andre had bedded everyone from star athletes, to big time Wall Street Executives. To him it didn't matter. If he liked your conversation and the way you looked, then it was on. And Sean Clemens definitely fit his criteria. He was happy when the boss turned him loose so they could get photos of him lip locking with his fine ass.

"I just hope it's enough so we can be done with it," Malik said ready to push on to the next case.

"Oh, it's enough. I made sure that his fiancé would know exactly what team Sean really played for," Andre boasted.

Malik really didn't want to hear the details, but he knew that Terri would be happy that they could finalize it, so that everyone's focus could turn to handling the Foster case.

"Okay, have a carrier drop the photos off. I'm going to call Terri now. I'm sure your Christmas bonus is going to look nice this year," said Malik before ending the call. He then picked up the phone to dial Terri's number.

Malik didn't like the fact that she'd gone to the charity event without him, but he knew that when business called, Terri was going to handle it. He let the phone ring several times before her answering service picked up. He left her a brief message about the progress they'd made, and told her to call him when she got a chance.

He ended the call and began thinking of all the dancing she would be doing with men holding her a little too close. He groaned in frustration, and signed on to the company website. He would work on some unfinished paperwork to try and keep his mind off of Terri and her eager dancing partners.

# Chapter 7

The music in the large ballroom was playing loud enough to entertain and low enough so that the guest would still be able to have a conversation. The musicians were all decked out in white tuxedos and they all were playing white instruments. The waiters, also dressed in all white, scurried around the guest making sure they either had an hors d'oeuvres or flute of champagne in their hands.

There were huge tables off to the side filled with delicious treats and overflowing fountains of fruity drinks. Large chandeliers hung overhead casting a dazzling beam of light on the dancing party goers. No expense had been taken. Tonight would be a night that everyone would enjoy.

So when the room suddenly quieted, Ivy took a look around to see what had caused the stir. She noticed everyone was looking towards the entrance, so she turned to see what had caught everyone's attention. Her gaze landed on a young woman standing in the doorway and smiled. *Of course it was a woman*, she thought, laughing.

Ivy watched as the woman looked around

nervously. It was obvious that she didn't know many of the people here. Her hands were gripping her clutch in a death grip. That's when Ivy took notice of her dress. It was beautiful. She was sure it was a one of a kind. The way it clung to her and draped in a way to tease had Ivy wishing she had found it first.

The woman complimented the dress by having her hair lifted up in a loose bun high on her head with wisps of curls surrounding her neck and ears. Diamond studded earrings gleamed in her ears and a diamond choker covered her small neck. There was only one word to describe her…flawless.

"Do you know her?" asked Nathaniel as he slid up beside his wife with a cool glass of punch.

Ivy turned and accepted the glass. "Thank you, baby. No, I've never seen her before. Have you?"

Nathaniel shook his head before turning to look down at her. "Nope. But who's looking," he said smiling.

"Yeah, right," she said grinning. "You can't tell me you don't think she's beautiful."

Nathaniel didn't even glance back at the woman. "I only know woman that I believe to be beautiful, and that's you. Now if you're thinking that you find that woman beautiful, then im going to have to sit back and re-evaluate this marriage," he said laughing.

Ivy tapped his shoulder playfully. "Ha, ha. Very funny. You know I don't get down like that."

"I don't know. You were really checking her out," he said smiling.

"Whatever. I was only admiring her dress," she

said, peering back in the woman's direction. "It's absolutely amazing."

"Wishing you'd seen it first, huh?"

Ivy turned to him smiling. "You know me so well."

Nathaniel leaned in and kissed her softly on the lips. "I know you very well." He leaned near her ear. "Every inch of you."

"Mmm."

Ivy groaned as she leaned closer. When Nathaniels lips closed over her ear lobe, she sighed.

"Why don't we take a moment and go out on the terrace. I want to show you something," he said, placing his hand at the small of her back.

The white silk of her floor length gown helped his hand slide down low until he was just barely touching her ass. When they began to move in the direction of the closed double doors Ivy took a quick look down at his zipper and noticed he was already hard and ready. She picked up the pace nodding in the direction of different guest calling out to them. Neither of them stopped until they got to the doors.

Ivy pushed open the doors and Nathaniel made sure he closed them behind him. He grabbed Ivys' hand and pulled her to the far side of the balcony so that they were hidden behind two large potted plants. From that section no one could see them unless they came over to search.

Nathaniel pushed her up against the wide banister and pressed into her. "Can you feel me?" he asked in a deep heavy voice.

Ivy reached out and gripped his dick through his pants. She massaged his length back and forth dragging a slow moan from his lips. "Is this what you wanted to show me?"

"Yes," he said, breathing hard.

She instantly let him go, pushing him away from her. She lifted her dress high up her legs until he could see the white crotchless panties she wore. Nate's eyes darkened as he stared down at her pussy peeking at him from between the lace.

"Now that you've seen mines, how about you show me yours."

Nate didn't waste a second. He quickly unbuttoned his pants, and lowered his zipper. He slid his hand inside his black briefs and pulled his shaft free. His hand stroked his length from the base to the tip letting his fingers glide over the fat tip.

"Okay, now what?" he asked, intrigued by her wanton behavior.

Ivy lifted her foot and placed it on the side of the potted plant. "It's your party sweety. What do you have a taste for?"

Nathaniel looked her in the eyes, loving the way she was flirting. He moved closer, dropping to his knees. He leaned in kissing her on her inner thigh. He inhaled her scent and smiled. "This is what I have a taste for Ivy. I can't get enough of your taste," he said before diving in.

Ivy's head fell back as Nate began a slow attack on her pussy. His tongue eased all around her lips before he allowed his tongue to delve deep between her folds. The sweet sounds of his sucking and lapping, combined with her low moans, were heard only by the night animals in the garden. Nothing was better than getting your pussy ate by the love of your life, while gazing up at the stars.

Soon Ivy reached her peak and Nate took his time sending her over the edge. When her breathing finally slowed, Nathaniel stood and drove his dick fully inside her. Ivy reached down and grabbed his ass in her hands pulling him closer. Wanting to reach her core, Nate lifted her legs and leaned her back against the wall. This move opened her wide for him and he gave her his full length.

Ivy bit down hard on Nate's shoulder when she felt him pressing deeply inside her. The sensation of having him fill and stretch her was unbelievable. When he began to move in and out, press and withdrawing, Ivy tightened her walls around him. The rotation of his hips as he drove into her harder and faster brought her quickly to another orgasm.

"Oh, my God. Nateeee."

Her cries of passion were muffled by his tuxedo jacket as she buried her face against his neck. Nathaniel braced his legs further apart and pulled her off the ledge. She was now suspended in the air, her body dropping down with all its weight onto his large dick. Up and down he lifted her, grinding into her wet opening. All she could do was hold onto his shoulders and endure. Endure the thick span of him as she rode him to his release.

The moment his dick expanded and the first spurt

of his juice met Ivy's, Nathaniel was lost. He was in awe of the incredible fervor that was taking over his body. Ivy's body was clutching and clinging to him and it left him feeling on the edge of ecstasy. He filled her with his seed until he had none left.

Panting and shivering, they eased apart slowly. In the mist of straightening their clothing they kept exchanging shy smiles and loving touches. Once their appearance was back to normal, Ivy reached up and placed her hand on his cheek.

"You have an unbelievable way of playing show and tell," she said smiling. "And I loved every minute of it."

Nathaniel took her hand from his face and kissed her palm. "I aim to please, love." He leaned down and gave her a slow kiss. "You know I love you, right?"

"You better," she said, pulling him down for another kiss.

**** 

Nothing but the low humming sound of the one hundred gallon salt water fish tank that sat tucked inside the wall could be heard as Terri entered her apartment. She removed her shoes, then bent down and scooped them up before heading towards her bedroom. She dropped the shoes on the floor and tossed her small clutch on the dresser. She walked inside her closet and began to unzip the dress from her weary body.

The benefit that June had gotten her a last minute invite to had been exciting, yet tiring. She had only gone to get a feel of Nathaniel, but found herself fighting off unwanted advances from men all night. Her face hurt from all the fake smiles, and her feet hurt from being twirled around the dance floor all night. There was nothing like being doted on by a bunch of rich, handsome men.

Stepping out of the dress, Terri left it on the floor, too tired to even pick it up. She then eased her underwear down and left them right there next to the dress. Next she began pulling the pins from her hair, letting the soft curls drop down to her shoulders.

Standing in the middle of the room naked, she knew that she wanted nothing more than to soak in a tub of her favorite scented bubbles, but the mere thought of having to wait until the tub filled had her dragging her weary body towards the bed. She was just about to ease between the sheets when she heard the beeping sound signaling she had a message on her cell. She looked at the dresser to where her clutch sat, thinking it looked too far away, but chose to retrieve it anyway.

Seeing that the message came from Malik, an exhausted smile crept across her lips. She thought of his little admission to her earlier, and her smile broadened. She pressed the right buttons to hear her message, and then pressed them again to return his call. When she heard his voice on the other end, she felt a little of the fatigue leave her.

"Hey party girl. How did things go?"

Terri slid between the cool sheets and snuggled

into her fluffy down pillows.

"Not as planned, but I did learn a little more about Nathaniel."

"And what did you learn?"

"Well, for starters, I can see that he loves his wife completely. I also think he seems to be a very calm and collected person. You know, very smooth."

Malik twisted his lips. *Whatever.* "Did you get to spend any time with him?" Malik asked, dreading the answer even though he knew it would have all been work related.

Terri lifted her hand to block a yawn, but failed. "No. He was the keynote speaker at the event, and every time I tried to make myself visible to him, someone always seemed to be in his face talking about city proposals and what not."

""What about the wife, Ivy?"

"Ivy was right by his side every moment. The only break the two of them took from each other was when the Mayor's wife pulled Ivy aside for some girl talk."

"So basically it was a wasted night." *Why do I feel happy that she didn't get to talk to him?*

"No, not at all. I got to meet a few more high society people, and I got to eat delicious catered food, and drink top of the line champagne. Did I mention I danced the night away?"

Malik closed his eyes trying to picture what she was wearing at the party, but when he saw a whole line of men waiting to hold her in their arms, his eyes popped open. Jealousy, hot and painful, speared through him.

"No, you didn't mention it."

Terri smiled hearing the tightness in his reply. *He's jealous.*

"Well, I did. With lots of handsome guys."

"Is that so?"

"Mm hmm."

"Terri?"

"Yes," she answered in a sleepy whisper. There was a long pause and she could hear him breathing through the phone.

Malik was at a lost for words, which wasn't often. But he found this to be the case whenever he was around her, or spoke to her. His feelings would begin to burn hot and he couldn't think. He could only feel.

"I um...I missed you today."

"Good," said Terri softly. She let out a girlish giggle and ended the call.

Malik was standing on his balcony nursing a beer. He was still holding the phone in his hand as he smiled. *Damn woman is driving me crazy.*

## Chapter 8

The bright afternoon sunlight beamed down on Malik's desk as he scanned through the pages of the thick folder he had on June Foster, Ivy Wallace, and her husband Nathaniel. It bothered him that June's past seemed so clean. Not even a speeding ticket or an unpaid bill going all the way back to her high school days.

"No one is that damn clean," he mumbled to himself.

He found out that Ivy had been a virgin bride when she married Nathaniel. She met him while she and her sister were on a cruise with a few friends and later started dating when he was transferred by his job to LA. Nathaniel had a slew of women chasing behind him, allegations of him cheating on exams while in college, and two DUI's which he pleaded guilty to. However, June Foster was squeaky clean. Nothing even came up about why she withdrew from her political race.

Wanting to brainstorm his thoughts with Terri, he reached for the phone to give her a call. He sighed in disappointment when the answering service picked up. He left a voice message, remembering that she was at the beauty salon, and probably couldn't answer her phone.

Leaning back in his chair, he continued tossing around the information his team had compiled. He had told them that he wanted to know exactly how Ivy made her initial money to get her business started. What her parents did for a living, and where they were now.

He also wanted to know who June had dated in college, and who she was dating today. He wanted his team to be thorough with their investigation, right down to what kind of dog food they fed the five poodles the tabloids claimed the family had. Because to him, a lot of things weren't adding up. It just all looked so staged.

Sitting up straight at his desk to close the folder, the picture in his open drawer caught his attention, and he smiled. It was a picture of Terri with her head down working. The light from her lamp cast a soft glow around her and he had been awestruck. Knowing that he had caught her unaware, he'd snapped the picture quickly before shoving his phone back into his pocket.

Malik smiled and reached for the picture, letting his fingertips glide lightly across the glass. He found that he was beginning to smile every time he thought of her and wondered if the strong feelings he was experiencing meant that he was falling in love. He wasn't quite sure, because he had never been in love before.

Of course he had a black book full of names and numbers of women he had bedded over the years, and a few that he'd even seen on more than two, or three occasions. If any women got to see him more than once, he was in what he considered to be *'in lustful love'* with her. Now he refused to even open his black book. In fact, he'd made a mental note to throw it away.

The door to the office opened, and a short lady walked in carrying a sealed manila envelope, which Malik knew had to be from Andre. She wore cutoff jean shorts, a purple tank top and a pair of scruffy sneakers. Her blond hair was jelled up into a mohawk and her eyes were covered with a pair of shades.

"Is this the right place," she asked, looking around frowning.

"What does the name on the envelope say?" Malik asked.

The delivery people from the Red Tale Delivery company always asked that question whenever they delivered anything here, even though the damn name was on the door. However, this woman had been here on several occasions, and liked to be a smart ass by continuing to ask every time she came.

The lady snatched off her shades revealing her blue bloodshot eyes. She turned the envelope right side up so it didn't say swov.

"It say's Vows."

"Well, that's the name on the door isn't it? So I guess you're in the right place," said Malik, already determining in his mind to cut her ten-dollar tip in half for being asinine.

Malik slid the lady the five-dollar bill across his desk and took the envelope she still held. She cut her beady eyes at him sharply before snatching up the money. When she turned to leave Malik heard her mumble something under her breath.

Instead of asking her to repeat what she'd said, he decided to let her go without an argument. "You're welcome."

The woman had already opened the door and was headed out when she looked back over her shoulder. "Yeah, thanks for nothing."

Malik couldn't help but shake his head and laugh. *Silly ass woman.*

Tossing the folder on his desk, he picked up the phone and dialed Terri's number again. There was still no answer, and he wondered if he should hop in his car and head over to the salon to make sure she was all right. He decided against that decision.

It would be too much like invading her personal space, and he didn't want her to feel that he was over protective, or maybe even the jealous type. He smiled as he realized that he was considering a woman's feelings for the first time. He knew at that moment that he was indeed in love with Terri Powell. There was no doubt about it. *Now all I have to do is stop being a coward and let her know. Yeah, piece of cake.*

\*\*\*\*

Terri left the salon feeling like a new woman. It

was something about getting a nail treatment and your feet massaged that drove all the tension away. She was headed towards her car when she checked her phone. She saw that Malik had called her twice, but she wasn't ready to return his call. She had another plan that she was about to put in motion.

After talking to June this morning about the charity event, she found out where Nathaniel usually went for lunch, and decided to make a surprise appearance. She looked at her watch and saw that she had fifteen minutes to make it happen, so she hurried to her car and slid into the plush leather seat. She revved the car's luxury engine, and headed for South Spring Street, where the restaurant was located.

Terri prided herself on always being thorough with everything she did. She was surprised that Nathaniel ate at The Parish. It was one of the spots that she frequented on many occasions. The flatiron shaped establishment made you feel like you were on the glass deck of an old ancient ocean liner. It had been the spot where she had closed many deals when she first started her company.

As soon as she arrived she noticed that the valet drivers were not working the lunch crowd, which was perfect for her. Terri cruised the parking lot and saw Nathaniel's Infiniti truck parked in the distance. Things seemed to be working in her favor when she saw two women in a silver Lexus pull out of their parking space leaving an open spot right next to his truck.

Terri whipped into the space and checked her watch once more. Seeing that he would be coming out in less than five minutes, she hit the trunk latch, threw on the hazard lights, and then stepped from the car. Inside the trunk, she opened her little tool box and removed a screwdriver.

This was her first time giving herself a flat tire, but she was about to play damsel in distress, so it needed to be done. Lifting her arm, she came down with the screwdriver with all her strength, cringing at the hiss sound that she heard coming from her eight hundred dollar Pirelli tire. She tossed the screwdriver back into the tool box and shoved it out of the way.

Just as she'd hoped, Nathaniel came sauntering out of The Parish carrying his leather briefcase in one hand, and talking on his cell with the other. At first he didn't see her, and Terri figured her plan was about to be a failure. She was trying to think of something to do to get his attention as she watched him toss his briefcase inside the truck, and then slide in. But as soon as he started the engine and looked over to his right shoulder to back up, he saw her.

Nathaniel looked at the woman and realized that he'd seen her before. He also noticed that she looked as if she was having some trouble. Exiting his truck, he made his way over to find out what was going on. He didn't really remember if he'd actually met her, but he definitely knew that he's seen her before.

"Are you okay?" he asked in a polite tone.

Terri noticed the tie he had on and saw that Nate

was Alpha Phi Alpha. They were usually a group of professional men who were normally strong natured and very successful.

"Actually, no I'm not all right. I can't believe I have a flat. As much as I paid for these tires I figured they should never go flat," she said, pretending to be frustrated.

"So you thought they would air themselves up every time you got a flat, huh" said Nate playfully.

Laughing lightly, she shook her head. "I know it sounds silly," she said hunching her shoulder. "But, I just figured I wouldn't be having this problem. At least that's what the commercial depicted," she said crossing her arms.

Terri had already opened one button too many on her shirt exposing a nice view of her creamy cleavage. She had also given a little extra spray of her favorite perfume to her wrist and neck. So when she crossed her arms, her breast plumped up more, almost spilling out of her blouse.

"Well, I'm sure you have Triple A right?" asked Nate hopefully.

"I thought I did, but it seems like I used my last tow last year in Alabama and forgot to send in my reinstatement fee," Terri lied. She was going to counter everything he threw her way in order to get him to change her tire.

"Then it looks like you're going to have to use a dummy," Nate said glancing down at her tire. His gaze never even lowered to her breast.

"Dummy? I don't think of you like that for

helping me," she replied, knowing exactly what he was talking about, but choosing to act like she didn't.

Nathaniel looked up and smiled. "No, I didn't say you were calling me a dummy. That's the terminology used for a spare tire. Some people call it a donut, but I'm a Midwest boy, and we call them dummies where I'm from."

"Oh," she said, looking embarrassed.

He laughed at her lack of car knowledge as he began to loosen his tie in preparation of removing the tire.

"Do you have a spare or dummy?"

"Yes. I have something. I mean it's in the trunk, but I've never seen it. I just know it came with the car," she said, sounding like an airhead.

Nathaniel walked over and lifted the latch in the floor of her trunk. "Let's take a look and see what you have in here." The storage area in her trunk held a small tire fastened down with a net.

"Looks like you have a spare. I'll get my kit and get started," he said, walking towards his truck.

"You have a kit?"

Smiling again, he nodded. "Yes. Every driver should have one. It helps in emergency situations like this."

Terri looked down at her tire and then down at her newly manicured nails and frowned. *Not in this lifetime.* She figured as long as there were companies like Tripple A, she would not be changing a tire. *Hell to the no*, she thought to herself.

Nathaniel worked quickly and carefully. He had

the jack under the car, and the flat tire off quickly, especially since his bolt remover was electric. The zipping sound it made as he removed the lugs set Terri on edge. *This was going way too fast and he hasn't even tried to look at my breast or ass even once.*

Terri made sure she bent over several times in his face and asked several questions about the lug nuts, the tire, and the time length that she had to get it changed properly. Once the dummy was on and secured, Nate stood up looking for something to wipe his hands.

Terri saw the look of frustration on his face as he looked at his hands and immediately bent over in the trunk making sure she gave him an eyeful. She thought for a second she felt his eyes undress her, but as she turned back to face him with an old towel, Nate had the same frustrated look on his face.

"You should be fine for a day or two on this dummy. Don't go over sixty, and don't drive on it too long," he continued as he wiped his hands on the towel.

"Alright."

"You look familiar to me," he said, his eyes narrowed in concentration. "Did you go to Cornell?"

"No, but I think you were a keynote speaker at a charity event I was at the other night," she answered, hoping to make him feel a little more comfortable with her.

"Yeah, okay," he said smiling. "I thought I might have met you before. Well, things should be all good here. I have to be running along. I need to file some motions over at the courthouse," he said, tossing the rag inside her trunk and closing it.

Terri had to think of something quick. He was getting away and she felt like she had made a fool out of herself.

"Wait, do I owe you anything. I mean for your time. I can repay you with whatever you want," she said softly, leaving no mystery to what she was offering.

"Nah, sweetheart. That's okay. You don't have to repay me in any way. I mean, what kind of man would I be to leave a gorgeous sista out in this sun with a flat tire?"

"But I feel I owe you something for your help," she said stepping closer to him.

Nathaniel reached into his pocket. "Here's my card. Any referrals you give me would suffice," he said, giving her a another look at his pearly whites. He bent down and picked up his emergency kit. "Enjoy the rest of your day beautiful," he said before walking back to his truck.

Terri watched Nate return his equipment back to his trunk space, and then climb into his truck. When he started the truck and drove off, she was standing there still shocked that he hadn't even tried to make a pass at her. *June was definitely wrong about this man. So why would she pose such accusations about him?*

# Chapter 9

The sun was still beaming down on the people of L.A. as Terri made her way through traffic. She had the air conditioner blowing on high trying to keep her skin cool from the sweltering heat. The Arnez Anthony Collection sunglasses she wore sat perched on her nose protecting her eyes from the bright rays of the sun.

Terri decided to wait until she made it back to the office to speak with Malik. However, she wasn't quite sure why, but she felt some type of way at being rejected by Nathaniel Wallace. Even though she would never actually sleep with him, it just would have felt good to know that he at least wanted to sleep with her.

*Damn, was my lipstick smeared or something?*

Finally reaching Vows, she pulled her car into the underground parking structure and saw Malik walking towards the entrance. She cut the car off and checked her watch and knew that he was on his lunch break. He was carrying a white paper bag that looked to be from the Yang Su restaurant a few blocks down the street.

Malik smiled when he saw Terri parking and walked over to her car, noticing the spare tire.

"Hey, I see you had a flat," he said, fumbling with the hot bag of food.

"I guess you can say that. I'll tell you about it when we get upstairs," Terri replied. She slid from the car and Malik's eyes lowered to her breast. *He's checking out my twins,* she thought smiling. *I'm glad someone noticed them.*

"Well, don't get too comfortable. We're having a guest around two o'clock," said Malik as they walked side by side towards the door leading into the building.

"A guest? And who would that be?" she asked, looking over at him as she stepped aside to allow him to open the door. She didn't remember making any appointments.

"It's Lilah Thompson. Andre sent over photos today that may be enough to close this case. I have them upstairs on my desk."

"That's good news. Have you looked at them?"

"No. I really wasn't in a rush to if you catch my meaning," he said with an uninterested expression.

Terri laughed as she brushed pass him on her way into her office. Malik stopped at his desk and sat the bag of food down. He retrieved the photos that Andre had sent over and headed in the same direction as Terri.

Once inside her office, Terri slipped off her shoes and sat down in the plush leather of her chair. A sigh escaped her lips as she allowed the tension of the day to seep from her body. Feeling a little more settled, she sat up and reached for the mouse on her desk. The computer screen lit up and she entered her password in the window so she could check her messages and send June a quick update on todays events.

Malik came into the office just as she pressed the enter button on the keyboard to send the message. When she looked up to see Malik carrying only the folder she frowned.

"Where's your food?" she asked.

"I figured I would wait until we looked at the pictures and discuss what's to be done next, so I don't lose it all to the trash can. Yang Su went up on their prices and I don't want to waste some good Lo Mein to the garbage man."

Malik plopped the carrier's envelope down in front of her.

"Are these the photos?" she asked.

"Yes. This is what I called you twice about today."

Terri heard the sharp tone of his voice, but chose not to speak on it. Apparently he was upset because he couldn't reach her. *Tough.*

"I'll let you take a look for yourself and see if you think it's satisfactory. I think it should be enough to close the Clemens case," Malik stated.

Terri was finally getting some good news and couldn't wait to open the envelope. She instantly put her hand over her mouth as she witnessed Sean Clemens tonguing down Andre. Some of the photos were of them engaged in passionate kisses, but in other photos they were touching and groping. One of the pictures had her eyes bulging out. Basically, the photos sealed the issue on why she'd never had a chance with Sean.

"Damn, it looks like no matter what I wore to the gym, ole boy wasn't ever going to be interested in what I had to offer.

"You sick, baby," said Malik chuckling. "Can I eat now?"

*He called me baby.* "Sure. Go and get your food," Terri said, tossing the photos back in the folder and setting it aside.

Malik stepped out to get his food and came back quickly. He sat down in front of Terri admiring her beauty. She had taken the time to button her shirt back up, but it didn't stop his eyes from roaming everywhere else. Like her soft, perfectly sized lips, or the way she always tucked that long curl of hair behind her ear to keep it from irritating her. Or the flawless arch of her eyebrows over her sultry brown eyes. Oh, there were so many things to admire about Terri Powell.

"Did you bring enough for two?" she asked, trying to peek over into his bag.

Malik had a slight smile on his lips as he pulled out two large containers. Feeling happy that he was able to spend this time alone with her, he decided to have a little fun.

"Do you want some?"

It wasn't what he said, but the way he said it, that made Terri's eyes shoot up from ogling the containers. Her hunger for the food was pushed to the back of her mind as a totally different hunger took its place. The low sexy timbre of his voice sent a naughty chill straight down to her core. Knowing he was being sassy with her, she decided to play along.

"Is it any good?" she asked, leaning back in her chair. She let her tongue slide slowly over her lips, before trapping her bottom lip between her teeth for a brief second.

Malik felt his dick thicken in his slacks and inhaled deeply. *Holy shit. Did she just flirt back?* Not to be outdone, he carefully opened one of the containers.

"Would you like to try it?"

Terri's eyes narrowed knowing damn well he wasn't talking about the Low Mein noodles. *Say yes dummy.*

"I think I'll have some if you don't mind giving it to me."

Malik couldn't believe his ears. Not only was Terri flirting back with him openly, but she was doing so right here in the office. Usually she was adamant about it being all work while in the office, but today she was breaking her own rule, and he knew he wasn't going to let this opportunity pass.

"Then come over here and get it. Come take what you want."

Terri's bravado was quickly leaving her, yet she could feel the sexual charge rushing through her veins. She wanted Malik to make love to her in the worst way, but wasn't sure if this was the right place for it. A vision of her being spread out across her desk, legs wrapped around his waist as he drove into her, caused her cheeks to redden.

It was at that moment when Malik knew that the game was over. He cleared his throat and reached for his bottle of water. After drinking deeply he drew in a deep breath and released it in a quick rush. Feeling as though he was back in control of his hormones, he reached for one of the containers and slid it towards her.

"So you want to tell me about that flat? I know those are some expensive ass tires you got."

Terri felt silly and ashamed of the way she had just let things go. She should never have led him on that way only to punk out like that. She wanted him. She knew that. And she knew that he wanted her too, but was it enough? She didn't want to ruin their friendship on a one night sex marathon, only to feel uncomfortable around each other the next day.

Not knowing what else to do, she went along with the change of subject, thankful that he had done so. "Whew, don't remind me," she said smiling.

"What happened?"

"Let's just say I tried to get a jump on things with Nathaniel and get the June Foster case closed, but it didn't go as planned." She explained to him how she flattened the tire only to be disappointed that he didn't take the bait.

"So let me get this straight. You flattened your own tire somewhere in a public parking lot where

Mr. Wallace was having lunch."

"Yes," she blurted out around a fork full of noodles. She then took a sip of her own water. "You know, this Wallace character doesn't seem like the type to cheat on his wife. I mean, I was acting like I was ready to be served on a platter, and he held his composure. He was so calm and steady he would have beat a lie detector test," she said, confusion plastered on her face.

"Baby, this man is an attorney. He won't be so easy to fool," Malik said as he also shoved a fork full of Lo Mein in his mouth. Just as he did, they heard the ringer to the main door buzz.

"Looks like it's show time," said Malik as he stood up. He grabbed the cartons and began closing them. Then he deposited the rest of the uneaten food back inside the white bag before tossing it into the trash.

"I'm going to go freshen up. Show her to the conference room. We'll meet with her in there."

"You got it, " said Malik as he went to greet Lilah Thompson.

****

Lilah stood near the window in the conference room looking out into the downtown traffic. She was dressed in a light blue pants suit that Terri was sure she had just seen Taraji Henson rocking on Empire last week. Her hair was draped down her back in beautiful, long tresses, and her skin was a beautiful shade of caramel without a single trace of makeup.

From what Terri read in Malik's report the

woman was educated and came from a good family. She hated the fact that she would have to deliver her the bad news about Sean. *She doesn't deserve this. No one does.*

"Please, Ms. Thompson, have a seat," Terri said as she strode further into the conference room and took the seat at the head of the table. Malik quickly took the seat on her right side, leaving Lilah to claim the seat on her left.

"Thank you. I've been waiting all day to get this over with. I know something is wrong because Sean has become even more distant, and he hasn't touched me in months. I thought maybe it was work related, but I believe it's something else."

Terri felt that Lilah was right about Sean's behavior. It just was a little more complicated than she thinks.

"Lilah, I'm afraid that when you thought that your fiance was cheating on you that you were correct," said Terri softly.

Lilah closed her eyes for a moment, trying to stay in control. When she felt herself calm down, she nodded. "Go on please. What did you find out?"

Malik opened the folder that he had sat in front of him on the table. "What we're about to share with you isn't going to be easy to take in. It's actually very damaging information towards your relationship," Malik said, looking at Lilah intensely. "I have to ask you before we proceed if you're sure you want to proceed with this meeting?"

"Yes, I do. I want to know what's going on now,

not after I say my vows."

Malik looked at Terri and she gave the go ahead for him to proceed. When he looked down at the photos and paused, the look on his face showed that he might be uncomfortable discussing the information about Sean with Lilah, so she interjected.

"Alright. Let's begin," she said, pulling the folder over in front of her. "If it's any constellation to you Lilah, I want you to know that I tried pursuing Sean several times and he wouldn't take the bait."

Lilah began to smile. "Well, as attractive as you are, if he didn't take the bait, what you have can't be all that bad, right?" she asked sounding hopeful.

Terri didn't know what to say to that. She felt the best way to tell her was to let her see for herself. After closing the folder, she slid the envelope over to Lilah.

Her reaction was the same as Terri's had been with her hand covering her mouth in shock, but then the tears flooded her eyes and spilled down her cheeks. Lilah was lost for words as she stared down at her future husband kissing a man deeply. There were several photos of him with this man and she was totally staggered by what she saw. The pictures showed him having dinner, and laughing and touching as if they were old lovers. When she saw the one of Sean sucking Andre's dick in the car she turned away.

"Did they have intercourse?" she asked almost in a whisper.

"We don't have sex with our clients. We get as close to it as possible, but we don't cross that line," said Malik.

Suddenly, a look of anger came across Lilah's face taking the place of shock. "He looks so fucking happy with this man's dick in his mouth. What the fuck is wrong with me?" she blurted out as she hopped up from her chair and began pacing by the window.

"I can't believe I wasn't enough for him," she said, wiping away a tear angrily. She stopped abruptly and stared at them with a crazy wild look in her eyes, and smiled. "You know what? This explains why every time we would have sex he wouldn't be able to come unless he fucked me in the ass." She burst out with a laugh that sounded more like a high pitched squeal.

"I've been giving him anal sex, which I fucking hate, and all he's been doing while he's behind me is fantasizing about a fucking man?" she yelled.

Lilah was breathing in and out rapidly and Terri began to get concerned. She had seen women faint and men have panic attacks after receiving news that their loved one was cheating. Nothing that was said was ever enough to prepare them for the outcome.

"Calm down, Lilah."

"No! I can't! Do you understand that I kissed this man and he's been using that same mouth to suck other men's dicks? Fuck that! He's going to pay," Lilah said angrily, walking back to the table.

Malik and Terri glanced at each other. "Lilah, I

hope you understand that Vows doesn't participate in any court proceedings. So if you go forward and use this information for financial gain by selling it to the tabloids, we will deny any involvement on how you obtained the information. We are known for keeping our findings private, and we intend to stay that way," Terri explained.

"Oh, I'm not going to use this to hurt his career," said Lilah. "I'm going to use this to make him boost up the carrots on this little ass ring he bought me. You think after five years of being engaged to him that I'm going to let this mother fucker off? Hell no!" she said, reaching for her clutch. "Oh, I'm still going to be Mrs. Sean Clemens. But, it's the new Lilah he needs to be worried about."

Terri looked over at Malik, and they both had a look on their faces that said Lilah was not playing with a full deck. *But to each their own*, Teri thought.

Lilah opened her clutch and slid the final check across the table to Terri. She yanked a tissue from her purse and dabbed at her eyes. When she felt she had herself in check, she smiled. "I want to thank you for everything. Vows has definitely served its purpose," she said before turning and walking out.

"Damn. She was mad as hell," said Malik.

"Hell, I would be too if I found out the man I'd been sharing my life with, and about to marry, was pitching for the other team." She shook her head. "That's a hard pill to swallow."

Malik stretched his legs out in front of him and crossed them at the ankle. "What really surprises me is that she's still going to marry him only to put him through hell."

"I guess she feels it's the only way to get him back. Personally, I would just cut my ties and move on. It's not worth the time and heartache that's sure to come once everything comes out in the open." Malik nodded in agreement. "Plus the embarrassment she'll feel if this goes public. She'll have the media all up in their business." He hunched his shoulders. "Some people don't know when to call it quits."

# Chapter 10

Malik and Terri sat in Maestro's Steakhouse celebrating the end of the Clemens case. Malik was so happy the case was over, that he decided to treat Terri to dinner. To be honest, he would have created another reason why they should go out to eat, but using the Clemens case was more suitable.

Terri had always wanted to eat at Maestro's, but had never gotten around to going. Now she sat looking around the place admiring the ambience in the room. The low lighting and white table cloths on every table seemed to create an ethereal glow and automatically gave you a relaxing feeling.

Malik sat watching her trying to act unaffected by her appearance, but couldn't hold off his stare. The low lighting casts a soft glow on her skin and she looked wonderful. They had come here right after closing, even though she had tried to talk her way out of it. When he had said that he was either taking her out or coming home with her, she conceded.

*Look at her now.* He couldn't understand why she had never settled down and gotten married. He'd seen her go out with guys, but they never did stick around long. *Why?* He sat with his head to the side just watching her as she looked at everything around her. *What happened to make her stop seeing them?*

She was beautiful, smart, eloquent, and successful. *Did her success intimidate them?* Could be, but he didn't think that was it. She was sexy. *Hell yes, she was sexy,* he thought, narrowing his eyes. But she's gentle, and shy sometimes, and it's absolutely adorable.

Malik sat up straighter in his chair. *Why would anyone walk away from her,* he wondered. *She's perfect.* Yet, he felt it didn't make sense as he reflected back to the many dates she'd had, and how none of those guys had stuck around longer than a month or so. The gifts would pour in at an alarming rate at the beginning, but then later the gifts would stop, and the phone calls would end. Malik leaned back in his chair again and smiled. He then reached over and grabbed his glass. *Their loss.*

"Let's toast."

"What are we toasting to?" Terri asked, liking the fun-loving mood he was in.

"Let's just say it's a toast to a better future," said Malik, looking as if he had a won the lottery.

"I'll toast to that," she replied, hoping that Malik hadn't caught her staring at his lips. *I love his lips.*

After taking a sip, she placed her glass on the table and began to smooth out the wrinkles on her napkin. When she glanced up to peek at Malik, he was looking right at her. A warm blush rose swiftly up her neck and she looked away. She felt she needed to talk about something, anything, to take his attention off her.

"So did you put your connections on June?" she asked, trying not to let her nervousness show.

Malik noticed her edgy movements and smiled. *Trying to evade the obvious Terri? Okay. I'll play along.*

"Yes, of course. After the money was wired to your account I got right on it. So far, nothing pertaining to anything foul has come up. I had them check into her political introduction and there was nothing out of the ordinary. She had Nathaniel represent her in some real estate matters where some tax issue's had come up, but other than that, I haven't found anything pertinent to say she is crazy."

Terri traced the rim of her flute glass with her index finger listening to Malik. She was hearing him, but her mind wasn't completely there. She really didn't want to talk about June. What she really wanted was to run her fingers over his chest and up over his strong shoulders.

"She's just a weird one. I can't put my finger on it," Terri said indifferently, trying to keep up with the conversation. "I sent her an email regarding the first attempts I made on Nathaniel, but I haven't gotten a response yet. But really though Malik, this Nathaniel guy doesn't seem like the type to go out and have sex with other women. I mean, the first time I tried pursuing him, you can almost say I put my breast in his mouth, but he didn't seem the least bit interested."

Malik frowned and gritted his teeth. *He better keep his fucking mouth away from my damn breasts.*

"I'm not sure if I even want to give it another try

myself," Terri continued. "I was thinking of having one of the girls come in and give it a shot. Maybe Sasha. I'm thinking that if he gets a look at Sasha and doesn't bite, then the man's not going to. Period," said Terri matter-of-factly before she took another sip from her glass. This time from her water.

Malik thought about what Terri was saying. It made sense to him on a couple different levels. First of all, it would take the woman he'd fallen in love with out of danger of meeting someone else and keep her breast away from the mouth of Nathaniel. Secondly, he's seen Sasha, and Terri had a point. Sasha was black, Latino, and Korean. She was a ten on the who's hot scale, and on top of that, she had a banging body with an ass that you couldn't help but want to lose yourself in.

"I think that's a good idea since Sasha's in town working on a video shoot for some ex gang member turned rapper. She would be more than happy to make the extra cash," said Malik, agreeing with her.

"Good. When we get back to the office tomorrow we'll see if June replied to the email I sent. If she's not satisfied, then we'll bring in Sasha. Just in case, did you do the profile on Nathaniel yet?" Terri asked.

"Yup! This guy has a pretty repetitious routine. Almost like the American Gangster movie," Malik said laughing.

"How so?"

"Well, he jogs two miles in the mornings around the Beverly Hills neighborhood. Nothing too strenuous though. Then he stops at Starbucks for his morning fix. After that, he goes into the office for a few hours. Then leaves around eleven o'clock and meets with the district attorney in the courthouse cafeteria. From there he goes right back to work. But at five o'clock he changes his routine."

"On Monday's and Thursday's he meets his wife for dinner. Tuesday and Wednesdays he plays golf with his attorney friends and a few judges. Now dig this, on Friday nights, he rotates. On the first and third Friday's he catches the new releases at the theater by himself. Then, on the second and last Friday, he spends three hours at Bally's Fitness center," said Malik smiling because he knew his team had done a great job getting the information together.

"Doesn't seem like he has a lot of time for cheating does it?"

Malik looked at her like she was crazy. "Not true."

"Explain please," she said, leaning back, all ears.

Malik new a lot about juggling woman and proceeded to educate her. "Well, for starters, he has a lot of opportunities to slide in a little secret sex, like after his Starbucks fix. He goes back to his office. A lot of affairs happen at the office. Then after his eleven o'clock meeting with the district attorney, he goes back to work. Who knows what he's doing there."

"Then there's those days where he rotates his schedule. Remember, he goes to the movies by himself and then to Bally's. That's plenty of time to meet up with someone and get a little something something going."

Terri was looking at him with her eyes wide. She would never have thought to look at his schedule that way. "Yes, well…" she stopped to clear her throat. "If we really need to use Sasha, we'll have plenty of places that we can implement her. I guess we can play this one by ear," she said ending the discussion.

They both turned in the direction of the waiter coming towards their table with a steaming tray of food.

"I agree," said Malik. "Now can we eat? This damn Porterhouse is calling my name," he said, smiling down at the food being unloaded from the tray.

"You're so greedy," she said laughing.

Malik rubbed his hands together. "Call me what you want, pretty lady," he said teasingly. "Call me what you want." *One day you're going to find out just how greedy I am,* he thought, glancing down at her cleavage.

# Chapter 11

The lights were turned off in the office as June sat back in her chair and sighed. It was late, and everyone had already gone home for the night. The building was quiet except for the occasional noise the cleanup crew would make as they emptied trash cans or wiped down glass doors.

The only reason June had stuck around was to see if any news had come in from that Vows woman. The bright glow from her computer screen lit up her face as she stared at the email from Terri. After reading the email, anger rose hot and fast in June.

"Damn! I do believe that I've given my money to an incompetent bimbo."

When she had originally heard of the company and seen the pictures of Terri in several magazines, she'd thought for sure, knowing Nathaniel's taste buds for women, that he would undoubtedly go for her. *How wrong was I?*

She had even followed Terri to the salon, and then to the restaurant where she'd witnessed the silly bunny in action trying to lure Nathaniel into some extracurricular activity. Her camera had clicked away as she'd hoped that he'd bite. Now, as she read over the email for the tenth time, June knew she had to formulate a plan B. Something a little more hardcore than trying to entice Nate with another woman. *He's too smart for that.*

Men like Nathaniel always have secrets, and she knew his very well. But it would be too damaging to just expose the secret she knew. She wanted Nate for herself, so ruining his name would be foolish.

She looked over at the picture on her desk of Nathaniel and Ivy on a trip to some island. He was handsome. Viral. Commanding. There was no way Ivy deserved a man like him.

"She doesn't know how to please a man like you," she said, staring down at his image in the photo. *But he's hers*, her mind countered, taunting her. *Not yours*.

June bit down so hard on the end of her ink pen that she almost bit through it. She slammed her mouse down on the rubber pad as she racked her brain about how to blow the top off the whole mess. Nothing came to her and she started getting frustrated by the minute.

Irritated, her mind slipped back into the past. Ever since she was a young girl, her younger sister Ivy was always coming out on top and ahead of her. *Oh, Ivy this dress looks so pretty on you. Ivy you look like an angel today. Straight A's again, Ivy? Ivy, Ivy, Ivy.*

That wasn't how life was supposed to be. It shouldn't have been so unfair. That's why June had always tried extra hard at everything, but it didn't matter. Ivy would always seem to come out on top, out shining her. It was the same even as adults. With her failed marriage, her parents had shown their disapproval, and again Ivy was used as an example.

*"Why can't you be more like your sister. Why must you make a mess of everything. You couldn't even hold on to your husband."*

*"Why couldn't you find a nice young man like Ivy?"*

The constant disapproval was maddening. That's when June decided to try a political career. She knew it would finally be something that would make her step out and away from her sister's shadow. Something that would make her parents proud of her. Her political run would also have put her in a position to not only be on top of Ivy, but destroy her company at the same time. She wanted nothing more than to see Ivy suffer for once.

But it never happened. Her chances at a political career flat lined. And to make things worse, Ivy gave her a job working for her. She knew Ivy thought that she was doing something great when she gave her the position at the company. A measly low six figures a year as head of procurement was really the biggest slap that Ivy had hit her with.

June knew that the company was worth every bit of a few hundred million dollars and then some. She had stock options, but hell, stock options wasn't shit compared to the real treasure that Ivy had, and that was Nathaniel. June wanted Nathaniel, right along with Ivy's monthly cash flow in her bank account. *But how do I get him?*

Frustrated by her lack of an answer, she decided to give it up for tonight and head home. Just as she was about to power off her computer, it came to her. The first quarter award ceremony will be tomorrow night at Nathaniel's and Ivy's house. June smiled as her mind went to work.

She knew that she had one last chance and this was going to be the big bang. She was going for the whole show in one courageous move. She knew all she had to do was get that Vows bitch to make her appearance and all the rest would fall in place.

She needed to call Terri and give her the new instructions for tomorrow. Looking at her watch, she saw that it was late, but she figured since she'd paid a hundred and fifty grand up front, it was never too late for her to call. She pressed the button sending the call through.

Terri answered her phone on the first ring. She was still up lying in bed wondering why Malik decided to just drop her off and not come upstairs. She had asked, but Malik had refused to stay. He made up some excuse about having some work to get done before tomorrow.

Not looking at the caller ID, she pressed the button to answer. "Hello," she said, hoping that is was Malik recanting his decision and was now on his way back.

"Hello, Ms. Powell. Glad to see you're not asleep." June voice was loud and sharp in Terri's ear and she pulled the phone away.

"I was just on my way to bed. How can I help you Ms. Foster?" Teri asked, pissed that she didn't stick to her regular office hours. "I gave you my final report earlier."

"Yes, you did, and I wanted to tell you that I think you did a great job," she said lying. "But, I also need you to try one more time."

Terri had to do her best not to sigh into the phone. "Really? Okay. That won't be a problem. I have someone I can use for…"

"No!" June said, cutting her off rudely. "I don't want another woman. I paid for the best and the best is you Ms. Powell. It has to be you or no one."

June didn't want to use another woman because Nathaniel was a smart man and he would begin to get suspicious. Although he has women throwing themselves at him all the time, June believed another incompetent woman from Vows would just ruin everything she'd worked hard for. Like tomorrow's arrangements for one.

Terri didn't like June's demanding tone and was about to check her on it, but June spoke first.

Feeling herself losing ground, June quickly changed her tune. "Look, I'm sorry for the way that came out. I'd just prefer to only use you for this. You've already touched base with him and it would seem a little fishy if different women keep popping up everywhere he goes. Plus, I have something planned for tomorrow."

Terri's curiosity had her asking, "What's supposed to happen tomorrow?"

"My sister's company is having an award ceremony to show appreciation to a few key employees. Last year I noticed that Nathaniel really did a lot of heavy drinking during the ceremony because it was at their home." June went on to fabricate her story. "I believe that he slipped away with a woman in a back room, but I'm not sure."

"So what are you suggesting? What do you need from me?" Terri asked.

"I need you to make an appearance tomorrow at the ceremony. Of course, there will be a nice bonus in it for you. If he takes the bait, I'll have the proof I need to present to my sister. If he doesn't, then you can take your bonus and walk away." June sighed heavily for extra measure. "At least then I'll feel better about my sister's choice for a husband."

Terri thought about what June was proposing and figured that it couldn't hurt to try again. Besides, it was her job to go to the limit.

"Alright, June. I'll give it one more try and come to the ceremony tomorrow."

June smiled. "It's by invitation only so I'll have your invitation dropped off at your office in the morning by a carrier."

"Okay. I'll keep an eye out for it."

Terri didn't get a chance to say good night, or hear June say it for that matter, before the phone went dead. She lay back on the bed, staring up at the ceiling, hoping that tomorrow would come and go quickly. She didn't care much for June. There was something about her that rubbed her the wrong way, but she couldn't put her finger on it.

Rolling to her side, she decided it really didn't matter. It would all be over tomorrow. Closing her eyes, her thoughts immediately went to Malik as she drifted off.

****

June sat there smiling after she hung up with Terri. She was mentally putting her plan together step by step and new the next thing that had to be done. She flipped through the contacts on her cell phone and found Dr. Charles Johnson's home number.

The last time she had talked to Dr. Johnson he'd been upset with her. He had tried to ask her out on a date because of the favors he was doing for her that had him risking his license, but she had laughed. Dr. Johnson was a weak man, and she didn't sleep with weak men. Although he was good looking and seemed to have a nice body, she wasn't interested in him like that. Besides, her pussy only belonged to Nathaniel.

"Dr. Johnson," he said when he answered the phone.

June could tell the good doctor was sleeping from the groggy slur of his greeting.

"Sorry to bother you Charles, but this is June, and I need another favor," she said.

Charles rolled over and took his glasses off the nightstand to look at the clock. "June, are you seriously calling me at this hour. I have a meeting early in the morning. I'm sure this could wait until the morning. Good night," he said ready to hang up.

"Don't you hang up on me Charles," June said fiercely. "This is very important. I need some

Ketamine, and I need it by tomorrow."

Charles flopped back on his pillows. "You can't just call me asking for these things. If this stuff turns up missing, and they find out I've been taking it, I can go to jail. Beside, I paid you back for that favor you did for me ten times over. If you want the Ketamine, then you have to do something for me," said Charles. He was fed up with June and her damn demands. All she had done for him was put in a good word for his son to get into a good college.

Gritting her teeth June's anger began to rise. "Charles, don't be so childish. Look, we can talk about this later. Right now, I really need the Ketamine."

Charles smiled hearing the desperation in her voice. He reached down and grabbed his hardening dick. "I have some here at the house, but I want something in return."

"What?"

"You," he said seductively. "I want you June. Spread out on my silk sheets as I slide my dick inside you. You want the drug, then be here in an hour."

Charles slammed the phone down and closed his eyes. He displayed a wide smile in the dark as his hand continued to stroke himself. *If she comes I'm going to fuck her until I get all my frustration out that she's caused.*

He rolled over and opened the drawer to his nightstand. Reaching inside, he pulled out a small bottle of pills. After reading the bottle making sure it was his Viagra, he popped one in his mouth and sipped from the glass of water he kept beside the bed. Cheesing like a kid at Christmas, he hopped up to get ready. The first thing he would do is reschedule his morning meeting.

# Chapter 12

"That mother fucker! Did he really think I was going to fuck him?" she said out loud in the empty office. *What choice do you have? You need the drug, right?*

Her thoughts caused her to pause. She knew she needed the drugs to make her plan work tomorrow. Otherwise, it would all be a failure. She picked up the empty soda can and hurled it across the room.

"Fuck!" she yelled in frustration. She stood up and took a calming breath, letting it out slowly. "You can do this. Just, go over there and persuade him to give it to you like before. He's a pushover. He'll bend. He always does."

Feeling better after her pep talk to herself, she grabbed her purse from the edge of her desk, and left the office. She hopped in her car and peeled out her parking space in the garage, heading in the direction to Charles house up in the hills. When she finally got there she only sat at the entrance for a brief moment before the iron gates swung open.

Charles had been watching the security cameras for her arrival. His heartbeat picked up when he saw her step from her car. She didn't bother ringing his bell. She never did. She just rushed in slamming the door behind her.

June saw him standing in the hall near the living room. When he turned and walked inside, she quickly followed. She wasn't in the mood for his shit. She wanted what she came for so she could get home and get some sleep. She had a big day tomorrow.

"Where is it?" she asked, walking into the elegantly decorated room. Today she paid no attention to the black Italian leather furniture or the plush carpeting under her feet.

"Would you like some champagne?" he asked, ignoring her question.

"Charles, I'm not here to drink champagne. Where's the Ketamine? I don't have time for your little games tonight," she said brushing past him.

Charles sat down his glass and closed the distance between them. "I guess you didn't take my terms seriously over the phone, but let me assure you, I was serious about them. Do you understand what I'm saying June?"

June looked at him as if he had lost his mind. "You really expect me to sleep with you?"

Charles laughed. "No. There will be no sleeping tonight. I intend to fuck you until my dick goes down or you pass out. Whichever comes first."

June looked him up and down and laughed. She couldn't picture him fucking her until she passed out. In her mind the only man capable of doing that was Nathaniel. Then a thought occurred to her. If she did give him some pussy, then she could have even more control over him. *Hell, from the looks of him, he'll probably bust a nut in five minutes or so.*

"Fine. Drop your damn pants so we can get this over with," she said, tossing her purse on the couch. When she reached up to unbutton her blouse, he stopped her.

"Not here. Le's go into the bedroom."

June wanted to get the whole ordeal over with, but Charles seemed to want to drag it out.

"What's wrong with right here?"

Charles took her hand and started down the hall. "Come on. The bedroom is more appropriate. More room, you know?" he said, looking back over his shoulder smiling.

"Whatever. Can we hurry this up please?"

Smiling, he pulled her along until he got to his bedroom. Inside, the room was softly lit by only one lamp shrouding the room in shadows. June looked around the spacious room impressed by the large bed dominating the room. When she turned to look at Charles he was no longer smiling.

"I've wanted to be with you since I first saw you. Come here June. It's time."

Not wanting him to touch her, but knowing this was the only way to get what she needed, June did as she was told and crossed the room to him. When he slid his hands in her hair, she wanted to pull away, but stood her ground. The feel of his fingers gently massaging her scalp wasn't so bad. However, when she saw him leaning in for a kiss she leaned back.

"I want it all or nothing. You decide," he said,

holding still only a fraction from her mouth.

When she didn't pull back again, he moved forwards and met her lips. The feel of his mouth on hers was soft and warm and she was surprised that she didn't cringe. She felt his tongue touch her lips and she opened up for his kiss. Trying to fight the attraction she felt, she decided not to participate.

"Kiss me back, June," he demanded as he entered her mouth once more.

Doing as she was told, she began mating her tongue with his. Charles groaned deep in his chest. He kept a little space between them, careful not to press into her while his hands began to roam over her body. When he felt his breathing getting out of control he stepped back.

"Take off your clothes. I want to see you."

Starting with her skirt, June unzipped the side, letting it drop to the floor. She bent down to pick up the skirt, but he stopped her.

"No. Leave it there. Keep going."

*Great, now I'm going to have a wrinkled skirt to wear home.* She unbuttoned her shirt quickly and shrugged out of it, letting it hit the floor. Charles eyes darkened when he saw that she wasn't wearing a bra. His focus was on the dark circles of her nipples and he licked his lips hungrily. June frowned.

"Those too," he said, nodding towards her lavender lace boy shorts.

Drawing in a steadying breath, she hooked her fingers under the material and eased them down. When they fell at her feet, she used her foot to move them aside. She watched him gawking her and was shocked that she wasn't repulsed.

"Can you hurry up please. This little seduction thing you got going on isn't necessary or wanted. Just hurry up and fuck me so I can go."

Charles didn't like the way she was trying to ruin his moment. He knew she didn't want to sleep with him, but he still was going to try and make it pleasurable for her. But her cruel behavior and foul mouth had him changing his mind.

"Get on the bed then," he said, concealing his anger.

*Finally*, she thought as she climbed up on the huge bed. She lay back and soon felt the bed dip beside her under his weight. Charles didn't say anything as he snatched a condom and slid it on his already erect penis. Looking down at her smooth skin glowing under the single lamp had him eager to be inside her.

He slid his hand up her stomach slowly until he had possession of her full breast. He squeezed it gently before leaning over to suck on the perky nipple. He drew the tiny morsel into his mouth and then bit down softly.

Although she didn't want Charles, her body still responded to his touch. A shiver of awareness shot through her and she moaned. Pissed that she had responded to him when she had decided to lay there like a board, she blurted out her irritation.

"Stop with this romantic shit and just fuck me so I can go! You know its going to be over in a few minutes anyway, Damn!"

Charles froze from her words, insulted by nastiness. Already feeling the effects of the Viagra rushing through him, he smiled. He lifted his hips and slid his pajama pants down and tossed them to the floor. He climbed between her legs spreading them wide.

"So you want me to fuck you and get it over with huh? Fine. Lets fuck then June."

Before June could brace herself, she felt the head of his dick paused at the entrance of her pussy. With one swift move Charles entered her and felt her tunnel clench around him. He looked down wanting to see the reaction of his dick penetrating her.

"Shit!" June yelled, feeling like she was being torn in two. Charles's dick felt too wide and her eyes watered and spilled out the corner of her eyes.

Smiling in triumph, he began to ease out slowly before pressing inside her once again, this time even deeper.

"Ahhh. Wait a minute," she said, reaching down to push him back. Her pussy was being stretched wider than it ever had been, and she didn't think she could take it.

"I tried to go slow for you, but you didn't want to. So now you're going to take this dick June. You're going to take it for as long as I can give it."

And he meant exactly that. He lifted her legs over his shoulders, delving deeper until he filled her tightness completely. June was basically at his mercy as he drove into her over and over bringing her to a climax so fast that it shocked her and had her screaming out his name.

"That's right call my name baby," he said next to her ear. He ground in her methodically slowing down the paste giving her a chance to catch her breath.

When June was able to slow her breathing, she inhaled deeply, wondering what the hell happened. Where the hell did the wimpy doctor get such a huge dick from. She was about to move from under him, but she felt him still thick and hard inside her. When she looked up, he was looking down at her watching her.

"Are you okay?" he asked with concern.

She nodded. "Yes, I'm fine," she said softly.

"Good," said Charles, a half smile on his face. "Now turn over. I want to fuck you from behind."

A look of disbelief was on her face and before she could argue, he had slid out of her, flipped her over on her stomach, and pulled her to her knees. He gripped her side with one hand, while he used the other hand to lift his shaft to enter her. The shock of him entering her caused June to lurch forward.

"Oh my God!" she called out in awe.

He began moving in her with strong, deliberate strokes smashing into the back of her thighs with such force that she had to grip the sheets to keep from flying off the bed. The power of his thrusts moved her forward until her head began hitting the headboard, but he still didn't slow down or stop. He had a mission, and that was to fuck little miss prissy in a way that she would always remember.

The sounds in the room were a mixture of her shouts, his grunts, thighs pounding, and the occasional slap across her firm ass. Charles grabbed her ass and spread her cheeks, enjoying the view of his flesh merged with hers. When he heard her crying out from another orgasm, he knew it was time to change positions. He wanted to stroke her G-spot in every position until she became light-headed from all the pleasure.

June couldn't believe this motherfucker was fucking her like a pro. His strokes were given with such precision to her kitty that she was coming all over the place. Her body was now falling back to earth after her second orgasm.

She felt Charles rubbing her back and shoulders. All of a sudden, he wrapped his arm around her, and they fell to the side while he was still buried deeply in her. His hand ran down her leg to the back of her knee and then he pushed it up higher leaving her open for his beating.

And that's exactly what he gave her; a beating. Or more like a dick beating. Charles fucked June until she begged him to stop. It was after seven in the morning when he finally relented. He drove her to one last orgasm while she rode him, controlling the tempo with his hands and hips. But watching her come apart above him triggered his own release. Now he watched her sleeping in his arms, curled all around him. He smiled victoriously knowing she would see him differently now.

# Chapter 13

The light ticking sound of Malik's ink pen tapping against his empty soda can was all that could be heard in the office. He was sitting at his desk wondering why Terri had been quiet for the whole day. She hadn't said much when he tried to ask her about a consultation she was having with a possible new client, and when he asked her about lunch, she declined.

He was hoping and praying that Terri wasn't feelings some type of way about last night. He knew that she had wanted him to spend the night at her place, but he declined. Although they weren't drunk, he didn't want the first time they came together to be with her brain muddled with alcohol. However, the next time the opportunity presented itself, he wasn't going to walk away.

Looking at his watch, he saw that the day was almost over. He got up and walked into Terri's office to find her in her private bathroom. He stood outside the door and spoke to her through the door.

"Hey, is everything okay?" Malik asked, leaning against the wall.

"Everything is fine," she replied as she walked out

the bathroom.

Malik's chin hit the floor as Terri walked pass him wearing a black Prada evening dress that fitted her like a runway model. The material draped over her body in all the right places. It called for a man's caress and his palms itched to answer.

His eyes scanned down her long, smooth legs to the black open toe high heel sandals on her feet and groaned. When his eyes lifted back to her face, he noticed that her hair was lifted in an up do with a riot of curls framing her face. Jealousy hot and fiery blazed through him.

"Well, someone looks fabulous. Must have a date," he said, a sardonic smile touching his lips.

Terri caught the sarcasm in his voice laced with a small hint of jealousy. She started to make him pay for not staying with her last night, but she couldn't do it. Even though she wanted him, she still wasn't entirely sure what he wanted. Besides, someone needed to know about the gathering tonight and be able to track her whereabouts.

"Actually, you're partially correct. I do have a date, but it's work."

"Is it the new client?" he asked.

"No. June wants me to give it one last try at a home event they're having out at the Wallace place. It's supposed to be some kind of quarterly gathering they do to acknowledge their most valuable employee's," she explained.

"You know I don't like that lady Terri. Even though I didn't find out anything about her, I still don't trust her. It's almost like she hasn't got a past, and that's not normal unless you've served in the military," he said, worried for the woman who held his heart.

"Malik, are you being over protective?" she asked, smiling as she brushed pass him.

He caught a whiff of the exotic perfume she was wearing and groaned inwardly. Terri always wore scents that drove him insane.

"It's not that," he said, walking up behind her, touching her shoulders. "I just don't get a good vibe from her. Hell, we got paid. We did our job. So what else is there to do?" he said, not really asking.

"Well this is the last thing, and we can move on from this case as well." Seeing that he was sulking she decided to lighten the mood. "I was hoping that we could celebrate closing this case afterwards," she replied with a sly smile.

Malik smirked at her mischievous smile. This just might be the opportunity that he was waiting for. He reached up and tugged on one of the soft curls hanging near her ear.

"You know something? That sounds like a good idea."

"Yeah?" *Oh shit.*

"Yeah," he repeated, stepping closer. He leaned his head down and briefly brushed his lips across hers. The tender kiss was only a promise of what was to come, and he promptly took a step back.

When Maliks' head bent down and his lips touched hers, Terri was shocked and relieved. She had been waiting for his kiss for so long that she easily leaned into it. However, it was over so quickly that she frowned.

Malik chuckled at her displeased expression. He gently tapped her on the nose, feeling thrilled that she had wanted his kiss, and more of them.

"With that being said, I'll drop you off at the Wallace mansion, and pick you up when you call," Malik said tucking her hand through his arm.

"What do you have in mind for tonight?" she asked shyly.

Malik looked down at the sexy woman beside him and felt his heart beat a little faster.

"Guess you'll just have to wait and see," he said, playfully.

She sighed in exasperation and anticipation. "Fine," she said. She turned her back to him reaching for her shawl, smiling.

****

The drive to the Wallace mansion took them to the outskirts of Beverly Hills. The neighborhood was home to many famous people and the houses were some of the most expensive real estate in all California. The lawns were all neatly manicured and the tree's that adorned the properties looked as if they'd been imported from Belize or Madrid.

The Wallace place looked like a palace from the street. It was a huge brick design that had several high points like a cathedral. The guard at the front gate checked Terri's reservation and eyed Malik.

"Oh, this is my driver," Terri said thinking

quickly.

The guard eyed Malik one more time, and against his better judgment, allowed them both to pass through the wrought iron gate.

"Your driver, huh?" Malik asked when he pulled up to the long line of guest vehicles waiting.

"Sometimes," Terri replied, smiling as she reached over and kissed him on the side of his face. "I'll call you maybe thirty minutes ahead of time. I'm going to try and make this as quick as possible. I just don't see Nate cheating on this Ivy chick, and I'm really getting sick of June. It's almost as if she wants the man to cheat."

"Okay, baby, but be careful," said Malik seriously. It was something about the way that he called her baby that really warmed her insides. Terri looked at his handsome face one more time before one of the valet attendants opened her door. Malik watched her slip away into a night filled with silk, diamonds and money.

Terri didn't get a chance to really meet Ivy at the first event she attended because she had to focus on business. This time, however, she'd make sure to tell the woman what a lovely home she had. Once inside, Terri saw a lot of the same people that were at the charity ball, only this time, she saw a few familiar faces that she recognized from a few of the make-up commercials on television.

June saw when Terri arrived and hastily rushed over to her like they had been the best of friends. She ignored the slight ache between her legs from letting Charles fuck her into the wee hours of the morning. Had she known that his dick was that big, and that he had taken a Viagra pill, she wouldn't have pushed him to rush.

"Glad to see you could make it," said June, whispering in Terri's ear.

Terri smiled in greeting. *As if I had a choice.* "Of course, I wouldn't miss a business assignment. That wouldn't be very professional, now would it?" Terri asked.

She was shocked that June had on the exact same dress and shoes that her sister Ivy was wearing. Her hair was fixed in the same style as well. *Creepy.* It was as if June was an 'Ivy wanna be' for some reason. She couldn't wait to get home and tell Malik about June and how she was looking like the chick from the movie *Single White Female.*

Once the thought crossed Terris' mind, she paused. *What if June was indeed just as crazy as the single white female chick?* Shaking her head, she quickly shook the thought off when June invited her on a tour of the house.

As they walked around the immaculate house, June showed Terri every room, including her sister and her husband's bedroom. *That was inappropriate.* She listened while June rambled on about how Vows had done a spectacular job.

"After this last test, I can put all this behind me and feel free to love my brother in-law without any unfairness."

"I hope so. I can tell that your sister truly loves

him and he loves her in return."

"Mm hmm," said June, her comment lacking any sincerity. She looked at her watch and saw that it was time for her big bang theory to play out.

"Shall we return?" Not waiting for an answer, she smiled and escorted Terri back downstairs.

As they came through the back of the house, they used the servants' quarters door which led right to the kitchen. June came to an abrupt stop before opening the wooden door.

"What's the matter?" Terri asked. June squinted and placed an index finger to her lips. Terri became quiet and listened to the voices on the other side of the door. She heard two men talking and one voice sounded familiar.

"Okay, little Ms. CEO. Here is where you get to earn your bonus. That's Nate in the kitchen talking to the master bartender Ben. Ben always makes some specialty drink for these events, so I guess Nate has snuck away to get his taste on."

"June." Terri said in a low whisper. "How am I going to explain coming out the servants' door?" she asked confused.

"Figure it out," she said, and then gave Terri a little shove through the door. She then turned and headed back the way she'd come.

Her plan was about to play out and she couldn't wait. She felt that it should go through without a problem since she had called and gave Ben the night off, and now her own personal friend whom she'd hired, was taking his place. Administering the drug to Nate and Terri was going to happen flawlessly. June turned her sinister sneer into a smile as she pleasurably rejoined her sister as she awarded some of the companies' employee's with their bonuses.

"Hey, we meet again," Nate said to Terri when he saw her appear from out of thin air. He had already had two of the drinks that the bartender had mixed together in the punch bowl, and was holding out his cup for a third.

"Hello Mr. Wallace. This is a beautiful home you have here. I must have gotten lost looking for an available ladies room," Terri replied.

"Oh, don't worry about that. It happens all the time. Come try one of these drinks my friend over here made. I love them," said Nate as he enthusiastically shoved a glass in her hand.

Terri took a sip of the drink cautiously expecting to taste a mouth full of strong liquor. She was surprised at the smooth, fruity taste.

"Wow. This is really good," she said drinking half the glass. *Damn this is really good,* she thought as she finished her drink.

It didn't take long for the mixture to affect Terri. She wasn't a big drinker so her tolerance levels couldn't handle much. June's planted friend smiled as he gave them both an evil chuckle before watching as they both collapsed to the floor.

The earpiece in Junes right ear went off. "Plan transport is now in action."

She smiled and clapped with the rest of the guests as Ivy continued to shovel out bonuses all the while looking around the room for her husband.

It wasn't long before Ivy realized that Nathaniel was nowhere to be found. She looked all over the house, and when she went to the garage, she noticed that his vehicle was gone. Back inside, she stepped into her private office, leaving everyone to party alone without her. June watched from a distance as her sister began to panic looking for her husband.

*Nathaniel where the hell are you?* Ivy dialed his cell number, but she continued getting his voice mail after the first ring. She didn't know what was wrong. He had never skipped out on a party before leaving her to host alone. Why now?

She tried calling his office to see if an emergency had come up that would have caused him to leave, but the after hour service answered, and assured her that no emergency calls had come in to the firm. Ivy was puzzled and frustrated. She had felt something was bothering Nathaniel lately, but he had refused to talk about it. He kept saying that work was overwhelming and it wasn't anything he couldn't handle.

Ivy had enough. She went back into her living room and dismissed her entire staff. June was now the only person there with her.

"Ivy, are you alright? You seemed a little brisk with ending the party. Is something wrong?" asked June, masking her face with concern.

"Its Nathaniel," she said, feeling insecure.

"What about him?"

Ivy shook her head slowly, her hair catching the

light and glowing beautifully. "I can't find him."

*Even when she's upset and unsettled she still manages to look fucking beautiful.* "What do you mean you can't find him?"

"I mean, I've searched all over the house and he isn't here. I checked to see if his car was still here, but it's gone." Her voice had a slight panic pitch to it.

June pretended to console her. "I'm sure there's a valid explanation Ivy. Maybe he got called into work."

"No. I called there too, and no emergencies have been reported."

"Hmm," said June, pretending to be worried. "This doesn't seem like Nate, but you know a man can be a man," she said continuing to throw doubt her way.

Her comment made Ivy think that maybe something fishy was going on. He has been a little distracted lately, especially in the bedroom. Normally they would have sex three to four times a week, but now it had dwindled down to about once a week. That night at the charity ball was so out of the norm, yet needed. She thought it had put everything back in order, but he was still distracted. *I need time to think.*

"Look June, why don't you just go on home. If something comes up and I need you, I'll call you," said Ivy dismissing her.

"Are you sure? I don't feel right leaving you alone like this," she lied.

"I'm a big girl June. I'll be alright."

"Okay then. Call me if you need anything. Understand?"

Ivy nodded, wanly smiling.

June gave her a brief hug and headed for the door.

****

Ivy tossed and turned all night rubbing Nates' side of the bed. *Was June right? Was it another woman that had him distracted? If it was another woman, then who?* There wasn't a woman in Los Angles that could measure up to her worth, so who in the hell could have won the attention of her man.

June's comment bounced from side to side in her head. *A man is still a man.* It made Ivy reflect back to June's first husband who strangely disappeared about two years ago. Later, a photo surfaced of him on a boat with a younger woman. Ivy remembered when June saw the picture, and her exact words were, '*A man is still a man.*'

Feeling completely drained from crying, Ivy finally dozed off in a fitful slumber.

## Chapter 14

The ringing of the doorbell woke Ivy early the next morning. Her head felt groggy from a restless night, but that didn't stop her from jumping up. She was hoping that it was Nathaniel and that he had come home with a logical excuse for leaving the party and staying out all night.

She was looking for a nightgown thinking that maybe he had received a business call the firm hadn't gotten. Maybe it had been something serious like he'd gotten mugged, or he had been held for ransom like they did on those television shows. A million silly thoughts ran through Ivy's head as she slid a nightgown over her head. She grabbed her silk robe and wrapped it securely around her waist. She couldn't wait to fling the door open and hear what he had to say for himself.

When Ivy finally reached downstairs and opened the door, the anticipation of seeing Nate standing there was wiped away when she saw it was June. June pranced past her looking like early morning sunshine while Ivy looked like something the cat dragged in.

*Bitch hasn't slept a wink huh? Not so beautiful today are we?*

"Hey girl. So where is my brother-in-law. I want to give him a piece of my mind for pulling such a horrible stunt yesterday."

Ivy closed the door after June whipped pass her. "He isn't home. He never came back," she said reluctantly.

"Oh, hell no!" June snapped. "He hasn't called all night?" she asked, already knowing the answer to that because she'd had one of her men discard his cell phone. Also, her bartender friend said they had consumed a lot of the mixture and they would be out until about noon.

"Have you contacted Lo Jack to see where his car is located?" June asked. She could tell from the stupid surprised look on Ivy's face that she hadn't even thought about that.

"I can do better than that," Ivy said as she walked over to the coffee table where her laptop was.

She sat down on the couch and powered it up quickly. Scrolling the desktop, she found the Lo Jack app that Nate showed her how to work. His vin number was in another file with all of their other vehicle's numbers. Ivy copied and pasted the vehicle identification number into the proper box and seconds later she had the whereabouts of her husbands car. Tears filled her eyes as the location revealed that Nate's car was parked in a Motel 6 on the outskirts of the city.

June sat next to her and peered at the computer

already knowing Nathaniel's location. "I can go with you if you want me to Ivy."

Ivy shook her head declining Junes offer. "No. I can do this alone." *Can I? Will I be able to face what I find?*

"Are you sure?" June asked, placing her hand on her shoulder in support.

"Yes, I'm sure," she said standing.

June stood as well and took Ivys' hand in hers. "Maybe it's nothing. Maybe he got drunk and pulled over to sleep it off so he wouldn't have to drive drunk. It could be a lot of things Ivy."

"Or maybe it's the one thing you haven't mentioned," Ivy said looking worried. When June didn't respond, she smiled sadly. "Don't worry about me. I'm just rambling on about nothing. I'll call you and let you know what I find out."

"Make sure you do," said June as she hugged her tightly.

She left the house, and as she walked down the steps she had a bright smile on her face, happy for once that things were turning in her favor.

Inside the house Ivy felt like someone had kicked her in the stomach. She had almost broke down and cried when she seen that Nathaniel's car was at a motel. She slowly walked down the hall trying to make sense of what was going on. *But none of this makes sense*, she thought. Yet, the only way to get answers was to get to that motel and ask questions.

Ivy ran up the stairs, careful not to trip on the smooth marble. She snatched a pair of jeans from the closet and slid into them. She then pulled an old college t-shirt on, and slid her feet into a pair of jogging shoes. She grabbed her hair up in a ponytail incase there was some drama from some unidentified woman. After getting dressed, she grabbed her purse and keys, and left the mansion heading in the direction of the cheap motel.

Ivy drove listlessly weaving through traffic like she was an Indy car driver. When she finally made it to the motel she drove through the parking lot searching for Nathaniels truck. When she saw it parked near the end of the lot, her chest constricted with pain.

"What are you doing here Nathaniel?" she whispered softly.

She looked around the area and was saddened by its condition. There was trash on the streets, and abandoned cars that had gotten stripped was left in the motel's lot. There was a group of men drinking and laughing loudly while lounging on an old couch.

"Why would he come here?"

Needing to know the answers to her questions, she found a parking space at the front entrance and pulled in. Climbing out of her sleek red Porche, Ivy was skeptical about leaving it. She made sure her alarm was activated before she made her way inside the motel and over to the front desk.

Inside the motel she cringed a little seeing how untidy and depressing the place was. The place was definitely old and needed major work, or be torn down. She wondered again why Nathaniel would come all the way out here to have an affair? *If he was having an affair,* she thought, trying to be optimistic.

There was a young girl behind the counter with her back to her. She was dancing to the music blaring from the earbuds in her ears while sticking yellow papers inside the marked cubicle blocks on the wall. Every now and then she would stop and do a dance move, popping her huge jiggly ass in the air. Then she would blurt out a few lyrics to the song she was listening to coupled by a few hip shakes.

"Excuse me?" Ivy called out trying to grab the girls' attention.

The music played on and her erotic dance continued.

"Excuse me, please," Ivy called out again louder.

When the girl continued to bop to the music, Ivy became upset. *What the hell kind of service is this?* Frustrated at being ignored, she stepped around the desk and tapped the girl on the shoulder.

The girl spun around holding her hand against her chest. "What the fuck! What'chu doing being the counter? You not supposed to be behind here."

Ivy stepped back and returned to her place on the other side of the desk. "I'm sorry. I was calling out to you, but you didn't hear me."

"Well, duh. That's because I was listening to my shit. What'chu need?" the girl asked, irritated at being disturbed.

Ivy was taken aback at the girl's rudeness. "I um…"

"Well, spit it out. I got things to do."

"I wanted to know if you had a guest by the name Nathaniel Wallace staying here?"

The girl looked Ivy up and down noticing her top dollar designer look. She shook her head and frowned. "Nah, we don't give out that kind of information here."

Ivy saw that the girl was about to be a problem. "Why not?"

The girl placed her hand on her hip and sucked her teeth. "Look around Boo Boo. If you staying here you definitely don't want to be found. Shoo, you could be the Po Po or something. You not draggin me in no bullshit."

Ivy smiled. "No, you don't understand," she said, digging in her purse and pulling out her drivers license. "He's my husband," she said, showing the girl.

The young girl leaned over and checked the I.D. and frowned. Suddenly, her whole demeanor changed. She went from Ms. Bitch to Ms. Understanding.

"So why you didn't check in with him? He cheating on you ain't he? And you here to catch his ass?" She sucked her teeth. "Man, dudes ain't shit no more. I caught my man cheating on me last week with Tonya. He talking about she like my little sister." She sucked her teeth again. "I was like, then yall on some real live incest shit right now then. He must think I'm stupid or something."

Ivy saw that bonding with the girl was her only chance at getting the information she needed from her. "What's your name?"

"Krystal, but my friends call me Star, because I'm always the center of attention."

That metaphor blew right over Ivy's head. "Can I call you Star?"

"I guess. I mean, everyone starts out as friends until they cross you, know what I mean?"

Ironically, Ivy did understand, and smiled. "Yes, I do understand. You're very smart, and perceptive."

Star frowned, thinking Ivy had called her a bad name. "Percept- what?"

Seeing herself about to lose ground, Ivy quickly corrected her blunder. "Perceptive. It means observant. You see things other people don't see. Like me being here because my husband is cheating on me."

"Ohhhh. Shit, I was about to say!" she said laughing. "But, yeah, I usually peep out stuff like that. You can't slide shit past me."

"I can tell. The thing is, I'm not entirely sure if my husband is cheating on me or not. I just know he's here because that's his truck outside. I'm here to get proof."

Star bit down on her lip with her crooked teeth contemplating. She turned towards the outdated computer bolted down to the wooden desk and tapped on the keys. When she read the information on the screen her face said it all.

"He came in last night with a guest. He's in room 2134, on the second floor."

Ivy put her head down. For a moment she was

hoping that Star would tell her that it was a mistake. That it was all a misunderstanding. Hearing the girl confirm it took her breath away.

*Why?* That was her first thought. Why the hell would he risk what they had? All that they had built together?

"That shit hurts, don't it?" asked Star, interrupting her thoughts.

Ivy had blocked out the girl's presence and drifted off, but her words brought her back. Anger, hot and fierce moved through her. When she lifted her head and met the girl's eyes, her gaze was heated, yet cold as steel.

"Yes, that shit does hurt," she agreed.

Star stepped back and hunched her shoulder's. "So what'chu gonna do?"

Ivy lifted her chin with renewed courage. "I want to confront him. To see with my own eyes. Ask him why."

Star smiled and nodded. She turned around and opened the locked cabinet that held the room keys. She pulled the key to Nathaniel's room down and slammed it hard on the counter.

"Go handle your business then."

Ivy picked up the key slowly and slid it in her pocket. She picked up her drivers license and shoved it back into her purse. She was about to close it, but stopped. She reached back in and yanked out a large wad of money. Leaning over she grabbed Star's wrist and placed the money in her hand.

"Don't be offended by this Star, but I want to

thank you. For everything."

Star looked down at all the hundred dollar bills in her hands and her eyes bulged. *Damn.*

"Don't worry. I'm not offended. You just be careful," she said, shoving the money in her pocket before anyone could see it.

Ivy smiled weakly, and walked towards the stairwell. Once she was on the second floor, she began searching for the room. *Room 2131, room 2132, room 2133.* Soon she was standing in front of the door marked 2134.

Leaning close to the door, she held her breath trying to hear something from inside, but all was quiet. She inserted the key in the lock and opened the door slowly. When she opened the door, she saw clothes scattered all over the floor. A woman's bra was slung haphazardly across a chair along with one of her shoes.

Ivy's breath hitched in her throat when she saw two bodies lying comfortably in the bed asleep. She flexed her fingers around the key she held in her hand as rage tore through her with a force she'd never experienced. *This son of a bitch.*

"Nathaniel." She said his name with controlled fury. When he didn't answer, she screamed his name at the top of her lungs. "Nathaniel!"

The sound of her scream woke them both. Nate rolled over onto his back, frowning. He dragged his hand down his face and yawned. Pushing up on his elbow, he peered down at Ivy and smiled. When he saw the fury in her eyes, his smile edged away. He was about to say something when he felt the sheet being pulled from his body.

Terri woke up feeling slightly lightheaded and disoriented. Her mouth was cotton dry and her stomach felt queasy. She dragged her hand through her hair, shifting it from her face. Finally able to focus, she sat up unsteadily. Under the sheet her foot hit something and she turned to see Nahaniel laying beside her.

Her eyes widened in confusion, mirroring his. Terri yanked the sheet up over her naked body wondering where she was. She began to panic at what she figured happened between them. *Damn, damn, damn!*

Nathaniel rubbed his head wondering the same thing Terri was wondering. He had no idea where he was, how he'd gotten there, or why he was in bed with this woman. But what he did know was that Ivy was looking at him with pain, humiliation, and worst of all…disappointment.

Ivy squinted her eyes, and if looks could kill, there would be two dead bodies lying in the bed. Not knowing what to say, she turned and ran for the door. She could hear Nathaniel yelling her name as she hauled ass down the dim hallway.

Nate stood up and realized he was naked, yet still tried to give chase. Feeling like he had caught a sudden case of vertigo, he stumbled and grabbed for the side of the bed. Palming his head, he shook it back and forth trying to clear the fuzziness. Whatever he had drunk last night was more powerful than usual.

Nate looked back at Terri in disgust. He noticed that she looked just as unsettled and confused as him, but he didn't care. He scooped his clothes up, falling down to his knees twice before he finally got one leg in his slacks.

Once he had gotten his pants on he reached for his shirt. He had shrugged his shirt on while trying to slide his feet into his shoes. He took another look over at the woman who still hadn't moved. She was sitting there looking as if she was trying to put things together, but couldn't. That's when recognition hit him and his lips curled in scorn.

"You! What the hell have you done!" he yelled. When she only looked at him in shock with tears in her eyes, he walked closer to her, leaning towards her face. He grabbed her shoulders painfully and shook her.

"I don't know who you are, or what the fuck you're on, but when I find out, I'm coming for you," he said threateningly. Before she could respond, he let her go and bolted out the door.

Terri cried throughout the whole process of getting dressed. She picked the now wrinkled dress up from the floor and slid back into it. She had to move slowly because her head was pounding and she kept getting dizzy.

She was too embarrassed to call Malik, but she knew he was probably somewhere worried to death about her. She sat on the edge of the bed still trying to figure out how she ended up in bed at some cheap motel with Nathaniel. It just didn't make sense. She'd already concluded that he wasn't the cheating kind, so how the hell did they end up here?

Closing her eyes, she tried retracing her steps from last night and the last thing she remembered was June telling her to go into the kitchen and give it one last try. Terri then remembered drinking something that Nate encouraged her to try. She remembered feeling dizzy, and felt herself slipping into darkness. But before she passed out completely, she thought she remembered hearing the man serving the drinks talking to June, but she didn't remember seeing June.

Suddenly, her eyes popped open. *That was it!* June had set them up. That must have been her whole plan from the beginning. *How could I have been so stupid?* How could she let June trick her into ruining two people's lives that were obviously perfect for each other. But more importantly, how was she going to explain this to Malik?

Feeling played, angry, and ready for some answers of her own, Terri hastily left the motel by the side exit. She remembered that June said that when she was ready, she could come out to her home to pick up her bonus check, so she caught a cab there asking the driver to wait once they arrived.

Junes house was much smaller than Ivy's. There was no security gate or large front driveway. However, the house was still large and in an upstanding neighborhood. Terri rang the bell and when the door was opened, June's butler looked as bored as ever as he allowed Terri to enter the foyer.

"Good morning Ms. Powell. Ms. Foster is expecting you," he said dryly. "Please, follow me."

*Expecting me?* Terri knew right then and there that June had used her. *But why?*

Terri entered the massive home office still wearing yesterdays clothes, and looked at June who was sitting behind a large glass topped white lacquered desk, clapping and smiling. Witnessing her response helped to put things into perspective for Terri. *The audacity of this bitch.*

Still clapping, June smiled widely at the woman walking into her office.

"June, please tell me you didn't drug me, kidnap me against my will, all so you could make me and Nathaniel sleep together to ruin your sister's marriage." Terri was livid as she confronted June. Her head was cocked to the side waiting for a response.

June waved her hand, brushing off Terri's accusations. She had already deposited the bonus money in the same account, but still reached for her checkbook to now offer Terri some hush money. She had what she wanted. She knew that Nate had no choice now but to run to her, and she'd be waiting with open arms.

"If I said no to those things you just accused me of I would be calling myself a liar," she said and laughed. "But my goodness, I can say this. If you ever want to go into acting, I have some connections. You deserve a fucking Grammy. You were so good," June said, tearing off the check. "I mean the way you were warming up to him in the kitchen was…well. Nevermind. It doesn't matter anymore."

Terri drew back as if she smelled something rancid. "You're a sick bitch June. I told you that Nathaniel was clean. That I did everything I could to persuade him, yet the man would not cheat on his wife. But no! You had to do this bullshit and set us up," Terri snapped, infuriated.

June laughed again. "You mean he wouldn't cheat on her anymore. And honey, please, you need to stop being so damn dramatic. You're getting paid well for services rendered."

Terri's fist balled up at her sides. "Are you calling me a whore?" Terri asked, feeling violated beyond belief.

June shrugged her shoulders. "If you are, then you just are. And a well paid one at that," she said grinning. "Make way for Terri Powell, from Vows. She'll do anything to close her case," June said, laughing at her own joke.

It took every ounce of decency in Terri not to haul off and smack the hell out of June.

"You're doing this for the money?" she asked, trying to make sense of it. "You want to take over your sisters' company don't you?"

June leaned back in her seat with a satisfied look. "Look around kiddo. Does it look like I need money?" June replied, realizing that she was close to saying to much.

She sat up straight in her chair and closed the large leather checkbook, and pushed the check over to Terri. She didn't give a damn what this slut had to say. Her plan had already been played out and it would only be a matter of time before Nathaniel came knocking at her door.

Absent-mindedly, Terri leaned over and picked up the so called bonus check. She knew what the money was really for and felt disgusted.

"Well, you've been paid Missy. You are dismissed," June said, turning away from her.

Terri was stunned. She stood there for a second starring at the crazy women trying to get a read on her. Then for some reason everything came to her as clear as day and her mouth dropped open. *Well, I'll be damned.*

"That's right. You don't want the money. You want Ivy's life. You want her fucking husband, but he doesn't want you. He chose Ivy. And you think that by breaking them up, he'll come running to you. Wow, you are one crazy jealous bitch," said Terri astounded.

June's face turned an ugly shade of burgundy. Her lips thinned out into flat lines smearing her flawless lipstick at the corners.

"Get the fuck out of my house before I stop payment on all the funds I've sent you." June angrily slammed down the ink pen she'd still been holding, fuming.

Seeing that she was on the right track, Terri kept going. "You used me for your own personal gain. It never was about making sure he was being faithful to Ivy. You wanted him, so you hired me to lure him into cheating so you could step in and pick up the pieces. You never gave a shit about Ivy," Terri said, balling up the check and throwing it at June.

"I said get out of my house! Ivy is young, she can handle it," said June, standing up. She leaned over and pressed a button next to her computer. Terri knew she must have summoned someone to escort her out.

"You're a conniving bitch June Foster, and I don't want any part of this dirty game your playing."

"It's much too late for that, baby girl," June said, sitting down smiling as two men walked in her office. "The game has already been played. And guess what? I won."

She spent her chair around facing a small wet bar behind her desk, and flicked her hand in Terri's direction. Both men grabbed Terri by each arm ready to force her out of June's office. Terri looked over her shoulder at each one of them letting them know she could walk on her own. They both released her, but stayed close.

Terri spun on her heels and left. Her mind was moving a mile a minute trying to come up with her next move.

*You think you've won. But we'll see about that.*

## Chapter 15

Terri thanked her lucky stars that the cab driver had kept his word and waited. She knew that she had to get to her office to speak with Malik, but she needed to make a quick stop first. She reached in her purse and pulled out her cell phone. After finding the number she wanted, she pressed the button. The phone rung twice before it was answered.

"Good morning, doctor Zuri," the woman said in a calm voice.

"Merilyn, are you busy. I need you to squeeze me in. It's extremely important."

Doctor Merilyn Zuri was a gynecologist, and also a friend. She had been one of Terri's first clients when she'd first opened for business. She had proven that Merilyn's boyfriend had not been cheating on her, but in fact was only working extra hours to afford a ring so he could propose. Happy with the outcome of her investigation, she and Merilyn clicked, and became friends.

"Terri, what's wrong? You sound like someone died," said Merilyn, dropping her pen to her desk.

"I'm on my way to your office now. I can explain everything to you once I get there," she said, wishing the cab driver would go faster.

"Alright. I don't have another appoint for forty five minutes. I can see you right away."

Terri closed her eyes sending up a silent prayer. "Thanks Lyn," she said, calling her by her nickname. "I'll be there shortly."

The drive over to Merilyn's private clinic took only fifteen minutes. Terri paid the driver and thanked him for his service before going into the building. When she entered the facility she was thankful that Merilyn was waiting at the front desk for her. They hugged briefly before Lyn escorted her to her office.

"Okay, spill it. What's got you so freaked out?" Lyn asked, her eyebrows drawn together with worry.

After taking a seat across from Lyn, Terri told her all about her new case without disclosing any names and the incident that took place that morning. By the time she finished, she felt a little better. Her hands were no longer trembling and her breathing was a little calmer. However, every time she thought about Malik, and how he was going to react, her stomach knotted up.

"Wow," said Lyn. "That's some story." She reached over and took Terri's hand showing support. "What do you need from me?"

Terri's eyes brimmed with tears. "I can't remember if we actually slept together. Or if we used protection," she said with a sob. "What if I get a disease or pregnant?" Her last words made her feel ill. *Will Malik still want me if I'm pregnant with another man's child. Of course not stupid.*

Lyn finally understood what she needed from her. "Don't worry. I'll run some test." She stood up and pulled a soft hospital gown from a drawer. The gown had little Tweetie Birds on it. "Get undressed and put this on."

Lyn then opened a cabinet and pulled out a plastic cup with a lid, along with a few long tubes. She turned and handed the cup to Terri. "Then go in the bathroom over there and give me a urine sample. I'll take some blood and then send all the samples down to the Lab while I give you an examination. I'll prioritize it so it will get checked faster."

Terri nodded her head, not able to speak. Lyn shoved her in the direction of the bathroom. "Go! And hurry up."

Minutes went by and finally, Terri emerged from the bathroom. She blushed when she handed Lyn her sample.

"Oh, stop blushing. It's just pee for heavens sake."

Terri smiled sadly. "I know."

"Get up on the examination bed and lay back. Put your feet up in the stirrups and cover your legs with the blanket. I'll be over there in a moment."

While Terri was doing as she was instructed, Lyn grabbed a pair of latex gloves and slid them on. She then used the urine sample to give her a pregnancy test. After setting up the test, she headed over to the examination table. Not even bothering to look at her, she pulled over a stool on wheels and positioned herself directly between her legs. She got busy examining her and felt Terri tense up. She knew just the thing to get her to relax.

"So have you made your move on that sexy assistant of yours? What's his name… Mike? Milton?"

"Malik," said Terri correcting her.

Lyn smiled.

"No, not really. I mean we danced at this restaurant and I made a fool of myself by drinking too much," she said frowning, but then she smiled. "He did take me back to his house though, and put me to bed."

Lyn looked up at her over the cover.

"We didn't do anything. He was a perfect gentlemen."

"Mm hmm," Lyn said knowingly.

Terri giggled.

"He kissed me yesterday," Terri said with a dreamy smile.

"And?" Lyn persuaded.

Terri sighed. "And then this happened."

Suddenly, Lyn sat up and pushed herself across the room on the stool rolling in a corner. "You can get dressed now," she said cheerfully, and then hopped up and went into her medicine closet.

Terri's head popped up and she watched her disappear into the closet. She eased her feet down and sat up in a sitting position. She watched Lyn's back as she moved around. *Wow, it must be bad*, she thought as she slid from the bed and went back in the bathroom to get dressed. When she came out Lyn was sitting at her desk waiting for her. She had a serious look on her face that caused Terri to swallow hard.

"Sit down Terri."

Terri sat down and Lyn turned around and grabbed a syringe. She made quick work of giving her the medicine and then swabbed it down before giving her a colorful band-aid.

"There, that should do it. Now, let me first tell you that you're not pregnant."

Terri sighed with relief.

"Also, I won't be taking any blood today. You're fine Terri. You two didn't have intercourse. You can rest easy now," Lyn said smiling.

Terri smiled and then stopped. "Wait, if I'm fine, what was the needle for?" she asked confused.

"Birth control," she stated matter-of-factly. "No mistakes, no heartbreaks."

Terri shook her head and they both burst into laughter.

****

After her visit with Lyn, Terri decided to go to the office and talk to Malik. She couldn't put it off any longer. She needed his advice and hopefully his understanding about the whole ordeal. She could at least tell him that she and Nathaniel hadn't slept together. That was good news.

The cab pulled into the underground garage. Seeing Malik's car let her know that he was already in the office. She instantly felt a wave of embarrassment as she paid the cab fare and got out wearing the same outfit he'd dropped her off in. Hopefully he would believe her and maybe even help her come up with a solution on what to do about June.

When Terri walked into the office, she was surprised at what she saw. Nathaniel Wallace was sitting in a lounge chair awaiting her arrival. Malik was behind his desk, eyeing her with an evil eye. Her heart felt like it fell to the bottom of her feet and she was stepping on it.

When Nate saw Terri he jumped out of his chair. Malik jumped up at the same time and stepped in front of him. He didn't know what Nate was capable of, but he still had only heard one side of the story. He wasn't going to let anything happen to *his* Terri. *My Terri?*

"I'm sorry Mr. Wallace." It was the only words that could escape her lips at the moment.

"Sorry! You ruined my damn life. My wife thinks we are having an affair and all you can do is say that you're sorry?" he bellowed furiously. His body trembled with the force of his anger.

"Hold up a minute," Malik said, giving Nathaniel a slight shove and a *'back the hell off'* look. He had to interject seeing the distraught look on Terri's face.

He turned to her blocking Nathaniels view of her. "Terri, what's going on?" he asked, softly lifting her chin.

Terri couldn't hold back her tears any longer. She broke down and fell into Malik's arms right in front of Nathaniel. She didn't care that he saw her crying or clinging to Malik. *Fuck it! I need him to hold me.*

"I don't know how this happened. That woman drugged us and set us up," Terri said, her voice muffled against Malik's chest.

Nathaniel's eyes widened. "WHAT! What did you say?" Nate asked, standing right next to the couple engulfed in each other's arms. He didn't care about manners or proper etiquette right now.

Terri looked up and met his stare. "Yes, your damn sister in law had that bartender drug us with that fruity mixture we were drinking," she explained pissed off.

Nate rubbed his chin and started thinking back to that moment. It hadn't been their normal bartender and drinking the mixture was the last thing he could remember before waking up to his screaming wife in the motel.

While Nathaniel seemed to be soaking in what she'd just said, Terri excused herself and went in her office and changed. When she emerged wearing a sneakers, jeans and a Dallas Cowboy T-shirt, she sat on one of the chairs in front of Malik's desk ready to tell everything about her visit to June's house.

After explaining what took place, Nate knew that Terri wasn't lying. He knew that June held a secret hatred for her sister, but he didn't know that it was deep enough for her to actually try this bullshit just to hurt her. He thought that once he'd helped her get her life back on track after her husband had gone missing, that she would find solace and move on.

But, then he remembered that he hadn't helped her willingly. Especially once he found out that she had actually murdered him. No, his stupidity and greed had him covering for her by photo-shopping a few pictures of her ex-husband with a young girl on a cruise ship.

At first he hadn't known that she had killed her husband. But once he found out, his agenda changed. He only helped her because he wanted to assist her in winning a position in political office so that his firm could represent more city officials and obtain the minority contracts for the construction union work. *I guess helping her get away with murder wasn't enough to leave Ivy alone.*

"Terri, you have to go to his wife and tell her what happened," said Malik, coming around his desk to sit next to her.

Terri knew that Malik was right. She had to make this right, and the only way to do that was to go to Ivy and tell her what June had done.

"I know. It's the only chance I have of fixing this," she replied.

Nathaniel knew that it was a shot in the dark. Ivy was still furious and was probably home with a house full of divorce attorneys ready to cut his throat. But, he didn't care. He just wanted his wife back.

Terri turned to Nathaniel. "Do you think you can give me a ride?"

Nate stood up abruptly. "I'm ready when you are."

When Terri stood up, Malik did the same. He reached for her hand and pulled her into his arms. She immediately rested her cheek on his chest.

"It's going to be all right," he said against her ear. "I'll be right behind you. I'll just wait outside the security gate for you."

She looked up at him shyly as she took a step back. "Thank you."

Malik nodded and smiled.

# Chapter 16

Terri and Nathaniel rode in his car to the house with Malik following close behind. During the drive, Nate questioned Terri on what her company actually did. After she explained to him what Vows was used for, he understood why he kept running into her, and that all of their encounters had been planned.

"Damn, June has quite the imagination, doesn't she?" he asked.

"If that's what you want to call it, then yes she does. But, I don't like the fact that she used me and my company to do some fucked up shit. That's not what my office does. We are not like that show cheaters," Terri said frowning. "We aim to help, not destroy."

"And by help, you mean showing women that the man in their life could possibly be a cheater."

Terri heard the sarcasm in his voice, and smiled. She could tell that he believed Vows only catered to women. "What if I told you that sixty percent of my clients are men wanting to see if their girlfriends, fiancé's, or wives are cheaters or are would-be cheaters?"

Nate glanced at her briefly before turning his

attention back to the road. "I'd say I've been thoroughly put in my place," he said smiling.

Terri smiled back. "Good. Serves you right."

They made the rest of the drive in silence, both thinking about how to approach the issue with Ivy.

Nathaniel's thoughts were headed in another direction. He was trying to devise a plan to get back at June. He couldn't believe she would pull such a stunt, especially after his helping her with her husband problem. He only helped June for the money and the fact that if he made more, he wouldn't have to walk in his wife's shadow of currency. That just didn't sit right with him. But first he had to try and salvage his marriage.

Half an hour later, they pulled up to the house and the security opened the gate when they saw Nate's car. He pulled up to the circular driveway and parked. Malik followed his lead and parked beside him. When Nathaniel reached for his door, Terri stopped him.

"You stay in the car, okay. Let me handle this," said Terri as she opened her door and eased out.

Nate looked over at the house and then back at her. "Are you sure?" He didn't know what kind of condition his wife was in and didn't think it was a good idea for her to go in alone. "Maybe I should go in with you."

"No. She doesn't need to see you right now." She drew in a quick breath and released it. "Hell, she shouldn't be seeing me either, but I have to do this."

Terri turned when she heard Maliks' car door

open. He stepped out the car and leaned on his door. His eyes watching her every move. She felt safe knowing he was here with her, and she dug deep and found the courage she needed to go in there and make things right.

"You got ten minutes and then I'm coming in to get you." When she looked like she was going to protest he held up his hand. "No debates, Terri. You have ten minutes." Terri nodded her head, accepting his terms.

Nate watched her walk up to the house and knew that Terri was one brave lady to willingly go in to see a woman who just recently saw you in bed with her husband. He wanted to see Ivy and make things right, but even he was scared to walk into that house right now. *Shit, better her than me.* After seeing Ivy angry at the motel, he was sure that his staying outside was the best thing right now.

Ivy was in the kitchen sitting at the island drinking a cup of tea when she heard the bell. Being upset when she got back home, she dismissed the staff again so she could be alone. When they saw the tears on her face, and how furious she was, they swiftly disappeared.

Now she was the only one here, which means she would have to open the door. She looked at the monitor over the marble countertop and couldn't believe her eyes. First she had seen Nate's car on camera one, then camera two showed that woman from the motel ringing her bell.

"I don't believe this shit!" Furious, she picked up

her favorite Ginsu knife and headed towards the door. Ivy flung the door open wide with the knife sticking straight out in front of her.

"What the fuck are you doing here?" she asked in a very unfriendly voice.

Ivy's eyes were burning holes in Terri and she took a step back when she saw the knife she was wielding. *Be brave Terri. Don't bitch out.*

When she first tried to speak, her voice came out in a comical squeak. She cleared her throat and tried again. "Mrs. Wallace, I need to talk to you," Terri said, looking at the blade imagining it piercing her lower abdomen. She was proud that her voice didn't crack this time.

"You don't have shit to say to me," Ivy replied raising the blade. Terri knew she couldn't turn and walk away, not without fixing her part of the messy situation.

"Trust me, you need to hear what I have to say," Terri said pleading.

Although Ivy felt she'd heard enough, her curiosity was piqued. Not about what she had to say, but what she had that pulled her husbands attention. She took a moment to check the woman out in a slow inspection.

The woman at her door was tall, shapely and beautiful. She wasn't wearing any makeup and still her beauty wasn't deniable. She had smooth, silky hair pulled back into a ponytail, her eyes were dark and expressive, shadowed by long lashes. Full, perfectly formed lips and a dainty nose made up the woman that had enough class and style to attract her husband. *She didn't just attract him. This bitch fucked your man!*

Ivy bristled at her inner thoughts. She continued to stare at the woman feeling that she'd seen her before, but she couldn't quite place her. Then it hit her. She was at the charity ball. She was the woman whose dress she had been ogling. *Damn.* Pushing that thought out her mind, Ivy was ready to end this so called visit.

She knew that Terri was bold coming here, but as bad as she wanted to cut her from ear to asshole, neither Terri or her cheating husband was worth her destroying her life. She figured that she better just close the door before she lost her last bit of sanity.

Terri saw that Ivy wasn't going to let her explain, when she saw her step back to close the door, and she knew she had to think quick. So she blurted out the only thing she could think of that would keep her from slamming the door in her face.

"It's about your sister June."

Ivy stopped and looked at Terri with narrowed, leery eyes.

"What about my sister?" she asked sharply, yet even more curious.

"Can I come in Ivy, please?" Terri asked, sounding as sincere as she could.

Ivy heard the sincerity in her voice, but hesitated. *Do I truly want to hear what she has to say? Do I really want this slut in my house?* Knowing that she had come all this way had Ivy wondering why. *That's not the behavior of a mistress, is it?*

Wanting some answers, Ivy stepped back to let her in. "You have five minutes," Ivy said coldly, still unsure about the whole ordeal.

Terri stepped inside the foyer and stopped. She wasn't expecting to be invited into the living room, and from the look on Ivy's face, she wasn't going to. So she decided to just say what she came to say.

"I know how it looked when you walked in that motel room this morning, but I assure you that Nathaniel and I were set up," said Terri. She saw the look of disbelief and confusion on Ivy's face, and continued.

"Your sister June set me and your husband up," she said, hoping to make things a little clearer.

Ivy's lips twisted. "Okay, see… Get the fuck out my house with your lies," said Ivy, walking back towards the front door.

"It's not a lie Ivy. Your sister drugged us and had someone place us in that room in bed together."

Ivy paused and turned to face Terri. Her eyes wide in disbelief and mistrust.

"WHAT?!"

"Please. Just hear me out as I try to offer some type of explanation. My name is Terri Powell, and I own a company called Vows. It's a company I started that helps people find out if their wives, husbands or fiance's can be trusted to be faithful to them before and after marriage," said Terri, pulling her business card out her back pocket and holding it out to Ivy.

Ivy took the card and read the information quickly. "Okay, but I'm not seeing where this is going, because I didn't hire you."

"No, but June did."

Ivy looked at her even more confused. "Why would June hire you. She's not even seeing anyone."

"She hired me because of you. She said you were filthy rich and wanted to make sure Nathaniel didn't just want your money. After trying to get him to sleep with me this past month…"

When she saw Ivy's eyes darken in anger, she held her hands up. "It's all part of the test. We never sleep with our clients."

She ignored Ivy's lips twisting again, seeing how she wouldn't believe that after finding her in bed with her husband.

"Like I said, after trying to gain his interest, and he didn't respond to any encounter, I saw that he was a good man, and faithful to you. I reported this information to your sister and she seemed genuinely happy for you."

"She then told me to come to your house and pick up my final payment. She said that you were having a party to honor your employees and that I could finally meet you. I was shocked that she wanted to introduce us, especially with your husband being there, but I agreed to come."

Terri could see that she finally had Ivy's attention. Hopefully, she was getting through to her even though it was a tough pill to swallow.

"The last thing I remember after her giving me a

tour of your home was us coming through the
servants corridor that led to the kitchen. Nathaniel
was there with the bartender testing some drink he'd
mixed. June told me it was the perfect time to make
one last attempt at him."

"She went back through the corridor, and I joined
your husband in the kitchen. I really wasn't going to
bother trying again because I was already sure about
my decision about him. I was planning on telling
June that I did, just to get the assignment over with."

"But then, Nathaniel persuaded me to try the
drink the bartender had mixed, and the next thing I
remember was waking up hearing your voice
screaming at us. I had a terrible hangover, but I
remember only having a few sips of the drink. I
asked Nathaniel what he remembered, and he said
the same thing. That's the truth, Ivy."

Ivy shook her head, turned, and headed into the
living room. Terri followed at a slower pace, mainly
because she was still holding the knife. Ivy flopped
down on the sofa looking like she was in shock.

"I don't know," Ivy said, shaking her head. She
ran her hand through her hair and let it settle on the
back of her neck trying to find a way to believe her.
"I want to believe you, but…"

Terri had only one card left to play. She walked
over and sat next to Ivy on the couch. She placed
her hand on hers and slid the knife from her loose
fingers. After placing it on the table, she turned
back to Ivy.

Terri leaned over and reached in her pocket and

pulled out her cell phone. After pressing a few buttons, she pushed the play button and sat the phone on the table. Soon, Junes voice was heard loud and clear talking to Terri about hiring her. After hearing the conversation, June sat there with anger clearly visible in her eyes. Terri could see that she now believed that June was involved.

"I can't believe she made you two sleep together to hurt me," she said quietly.

"Ivy, your husband is still faithful. Nothing happened."

"How can you say that?" she asked, looking at her with tears in her eyes. "Even if you both were drugged, it still stands that you slept together."

Terri smiled. "We slept in the same bed together, but we didn't have sex." Seeing that Ivy was confused, she went on. "I was so afraid of not remembering what happened, or if we even used protection that night, that I went to my doctor to get myself tested. I was told not to worry about a thing. That I was still as healthy as a horse."

"But that doesn't mean you didn't sleep with him," Ivy said, trying to mask her pain.

"No, it doesn't. But, since my doctor told me I didn't have sex, it also means that I'm still a virgin," said Terri smiling.

Ivy's eyes spread wide in surprise. She covered her hand with her mouth and gasped. "You're still a virgin?"

Terry laughed. "Yes. I want to save myself for the right one. Sort of like the one you've found. But, that's besides the point," she said smiling. "My still being a virgin means that Nathaniel and I never slept together. Whoever moved us just put us in bed together to give the impression that we had."

Ivy was smiling with excitement, but then her smile faded, and her eyes began to swim with tears. "Oh my God!"

Terri frowned. "What's wrong?"

"Nathaniel! I told him to get out and that I didn't want to see him any more. I said so many cruel things to him. My lawyers are drawing up papers now for a divorce," Ivy confessed.

*Damn, rich people move fast.* "I'm sure, under the circumstances that Nathaniel will forgive you. That man loves you. And you can always call your lawyers and stop the paperwork."

"How can you be so sure?" asked Ivy. The terrible things she had yelled to him over the phone when he kept calling, and when he showed up here, kept playing in her mind.

Smiling, Terri got up and walked over to the front door. When she opened it, Nathaniel was standing there looking vulnerable, wrinkled, and a total mess. He followed Terri into the living room, unsure of what he'd find.

When Ivy saw him, she hopped up from the couch and ran to him. She flung her body at him and he swept her up in his arms tightly. He rained kisses over her face, loving the fact that she was trying to do the same thing. It looked comical to Terri, and she shook her head grinning.

"Oh, Nate. I'm so sorry. I shouldn't have doubted you. I should have listened when you tried to explain."

"No, Ivy. If the shoe was on the other foot, and I'd found you in bed with another man, I would have caught a case. I wouldn't have wanted to listen to what you had to say either. I'm just sorry you had to go through this." He exhaled all his tension and kissed her deeply. "I was so damn scared you wouldn't take me back."

Terri was all for the happy reunion, but there was still a problem unsolved. "I'm sorry to intrude guys, but what are you going to do about your sister?" Terri asked Ivy.

Ivy stepped back from Nate, but he didn't release her. "Don't worry about June. I'll deal with her ass," Ivy said, turning back to face Nate, kissing him again.

"I'm sorry I ever doubted you baby," she said looking into his eyes.

Nate looked over her shoulder and moved his lips thanking Terri. Terri nodded and headed towards the door. As she walked out the door, she felt thankful knowing that Malik was waiting for her. Now that she had righted her wrong against the Wallace's, she now had time to sort through this thing she had with Malik. She was through playing the guessing game about his feelings. She needed things clarified and put in perspective.

## Chapter 17

June returned to her office the next day to prepare for a meeting as if nothing ever happened. She never heard anything from Ivy or Nathaniel accusing her of anything, so she figured Terri had done what she'd paid her to do and kept her mouth closed. Now she was reading through a few reports that required her attention, but every now and then she would think about Nathaniel, counting the hours until he would reach out to her. She was sure that Terri wouldn't say anything to Ivy about her involvement now that she'd gotten paid. Besides, Ivy wouldn't believe her without any proof. *It would be her word against mine*, she thought smiling.

With her taking the money, it made her look just as guilty, and Ivy would be too upset to even listen. And even if she got Ivy to listen, June would just deny everything. Plus, there was still the fact that she'd caught them in bed together. There was no way that bitch could prove that she and Nathaniel didn't fuck.

She continued to smile as she began sifting through the stack of papers on her desk. She was feeling better than she'd ever felt in her life. Who needed the path paved to the White House when she had now paved the way to Nathaniel's heart. Soon she would have Ivys' life and everything that came along with it. As June reached over and lifted the cup of Carmel Latte to her lips and took a sip, she glanced up to see her sister walk in her office without even knocking.

"Ivy!" she said in surprise, standing abruptly, wincing as some of the hot liquid spilled onto her hand. She grabbed a tissue and blotted the moisture from her fingers. "I didn't know you were coming in today," she said, breathlessly.

Ivy had gotten up at the crack of dawn pacing her living room as she debated on what to do about June. She had always known that there was a bit of competition between them growing up, but had always thought it was a common behavior between siblings. But now, after this bullshit she had pulled, she knew without a doubt that June's dislike had turned into something else.

She had gone through a great deal of trouble to try and destroy her marriage, and for what? Nathaniel didn't want her, so what was the point. That was the question that brought her here today. She wanted to confront her face to face and hear what she had to say for herself.

Ivy stared at her long and hard before she spoke. "How could you do that to me June?" she whispered in anguish. The pain Ivy was feeling in her heart was showing in her eyes. "You're my sister. My fucking sister June!" she said, her voice rising an octave.

"You're my own flesh and blood for Christ sake," she said sorrowfully.

When June didn't respond, only stood there with a blank stare, Ivy became even more upset. She nodded her head and quickly wiped away the lone tear that slid from her eye. Witnessing her indifference, Ivy's eyes hardened, and she released a breath through her lips slowly, letting go of the stress.

June was at a lost for words. She didn't have a response for Ivy, because technically, she never thought that she would be confronted. She couldn't believe that little bitch had really gone back and snitched on her. She got paid to do a job, and was supposed to keep it all confidential, but had run and spilled her damn guts. Now June was being questioned by Ivy and was totally unprepared. She was trying to muster up an excuse, but couldn't come up with anything.

Seeing that she wasn't going to get an answer from June, Ivy continued with their conversation. "Fine *sister*," she said with a sneer. "If this is the way you want to play it, then let me show you how this game is going to get played. You're no longer employed by Wallace Incorporated. You also no longer have a vote on the board that counts. My personal accounts, as well as my company accounts, have all been changed, therefore you no longer have any access to them. I took the liberty of cancelling your petty cash accounts as well."

"I want you to stay away from *my* husband. And I

want you to stay away from me. You have an hour to clear out your office and get the hell out of my building, because every security guard on my payroll knows that after twelve noon today, you will be required to sign in and will be treated as a visitor," Ivy said as she started to turn and walk away, then stopped.

"And in light of your being my sister, and my being a Christian, I'm going to do what I believe is the right thing. I have deposited one million dollars into your private bank account. That's all you will get from me."

June's eyes widen in disbelief. "Wait, you can't do this Ivy. What the hell am I going to do with a measly one million dollars."

Ivy's gritted her teeth, hearing how ungrateful her sister was. "You better live the best you can big sis. Because as of right now, I don't give a fuck," she said, finally turning to walk out the door.

June was furious. How the hell had she lost control of everything? She felt her life spiraling in different directions and felt sick thinking she would be losing Nathaniel for good. Feeling defeat rush through her with a sickening searing heat, she gave up her act of loyalty and looked evilly at Ivy, her expression showing her true feelings.

Not knowing what to say to Ivy's demands, she blurted out what was on her mind and in her heart. "You don't deserve him!" June yelled. "I saw Nathaniel first while we were on that cruise, and you took him from me! Just like you do with everything.

You always got to be the one who gets everything. He didn't even want you!"

Ivy just continued walking towards the door while June continued to scream hysterically, sounding more and more like she had totally slipped from reality.

"I would be a better wife than you! You're just a spoiled ass bitch! You're nothing! I'll get him! You watch!"

Ivy stopped in her tracks at the threat June just made.

"What did you say?" she asked, spinning around to face her. She closed her eyes briefly, shaking her head in frustration. "June, please don't test me right now. I will fight tooth and nail for what's mine, so you better be careful what you fucking say to me."

"And I feel the same way little sister," June said with a high handed laugh. "Technically, he really *is* mine. Hell, he's been inside me just as much as he's been inside you. But, you know how the saying goes. If I can't have him, no one will."

"You're a sick lying bitch," said Ivy angry. "He never wanted you. I mean, why would he?" she asked, fanning the flame of hate already burning out of control inside June's mind.

A strange look settled on June's face as she stared evilly at June. All of a sudden, she came charging from behind her desk raving mad to attack Ivy.

Ivy saw her rushing towards her and quickly grabbed one of the office chairs on wheels and shoved it in her direction. The chair banged into her shin sending her flying into the wall. Once June got her balance, she grabbed the first thing she saw; an electric pencil sharpener. She lunged it at Ivy's head missing her only by an inch.

"Bitch are you crazy!" yelled Ivy as she watched the device shatter when it hit the floor.

Before Ivy could say anything else, June reached out and slapped her in the face. Ivy may have been a lot smaller than June, but she packed a mean right hook. Her first blow caught June square on the jaw rocking her backwards. June tasted the blood in the corner of her mouth and smiled a sick grin.

"Did you forget who use to fight your battles for you," she asked Ivy before connecting a right of her own.

The fight had Ivy's adrenaline pumping at an accelerated pace. June had always been good with her hands, but Ivy refused to let her get the best of her. They locked in a bear hug and June begun pulling her hair.

They ended up slumped against a table that held a fax machine and a small copier. Ivy was banging June's head into the desk with force, and June's eyes were desperately darting around for a new weapon. Her hand reached up above her head and the only thing she felt was the telephone wire to the fax machine. She yanked the wires free and swiftly wrapped them around Ivy's neck. Once she began twisting, Ivy let go of her hair and grabbed for the cord around her throat.

"Can't breathe, huh?" asked June furiously as she

fought to hold her grip.

Ivy twisted her body, causing June to lean into her. She then threw all her weight back just enough to reach down and lift the paper weight. With all her might she smashed it into June's face. The pain caused June to release one hand from the cord and grab her throbbing head. As soon as Ivy felt the cord loosen, she leaned forward, lifting June off her feet, and flipping her to the floor.

June released the cord so she could brace herself for the fall. She hit the floor with a loud thud that pushed all the air from her lungs. Ivy saw June trying to get up and shoved the fax machine off the table towards her. At the last minute, June rolled out of harms way and the machine only grazed her shoulder.

In an attempt to get revenge, June reached for the metal garbage can and cracked Ivy in the knee. She then tried to grab Ivy by the throat, but Ivy got her hands around June's neck first. She raised her knee and with a strong blow, rammed her knee into June's pussy.

"Oh, fuck!" June cried out in pain and fell to the floor.

"I guess that shit works on bitches too, huh?" said Ivy, wiping a splatter of blood from her lip.

She stood there breathing heavy and looking down at June curled up in a ball with her hands planted between her legs. Thinking that the fight was over, she shook her head in disgust, and began to walk away, leaving June on the floor.

Seeing her back turned, June slowly got up and attacked her again.

Ivy glance back just as June slammed her fist in her face. The blow had her seeing stars, but she was still able to grab a fist full of June hair. She took her free hand and dug her nails into June's right eye and she yelped in pain.

Trying to shake Ivy loose, she grabbed a fist full of hair as well, and shoved her hard. They landed on a smoked glass coffee table in June's office. The weight of their bodies caused it to shatter into four huge thick pieces with tiny shards splintering everywhere.

Ivy felt June's grip in her hair loosen and she hopped to her feet ready to continue the battle. That's when she noticed the red spot widening quickly on her sister's yellow blouse. She almost fainted when she saw a thick piece of glass lodged in June's side protruding through the material.

As much as Ivy hated what June had done, and even though they had done the unthinkable by physically fighting each other, deep down she still loved her sister. She didn't want to see her lying there in pain, her life's blood slowly staining the floor. Dropping down to her knees, she looked down at June in horror.

"June! Oh my God."

Her hands hovered over her body not knowing where to touch her. Finally, her mind began to work and she shakily got back to her feet and ran over to June's desk. She began to cry as she picked up the phone and dialed the police.

"911 what's your emergency?" asked the dispatcher.

"My name is Ivy Wallace. I'm at 1743 Milcrest Boulevard on the seventeenth floor. My sister fell on a table and she has a large piece of glass sticking through her side. She's bleeding profusely. Please send an ambulance."

"Okay, Mam. I need a little more information from you."

After giving the woman the details, Ivy laid the phone on her desk without hanging it up. She didn't have time to have a conversation with the woman. She gave the address, so all she needed to do was send someone. She needed to be by her sister's side.

Ivy returned to June and again kneeled down beside her. She took June's now bloody hand in hers and held on tightly. "I called for an ambulance sis. Just hold on okay. They'll be here soon."

Ivy kept talking to June, not giving her a chance to pass out or drift off. The dispatcher did her job and sent a medic unit to the company. As soon as they arrived and assessed the damage, they began administering care to June. While they were working on June, Ivy took the time to call Nathaniel.

"Hey baby, what's up. You were gone when I woke up," he said, smiling, remembering their night of lovemaking.

"Nate, something's happened."

From the tone of her voice Nathaniel knew it was something serious. "Where are you?"

"I'm at the Wallace Building. June and I got into a fight and we fell. There's so much blood, and it's on my hands," she said crying.

*What the fuck?* "Shit! Who's with you? Where's Anthony?" he asked, wondering where the head of security was?

"I don't know. Nate, I need you," she said, her voice nothing but a whisper.

"Don't worry baby. I'm already on my way. I should be there in a few minutes. Stay on the line with me, okay?"

"Okay."

Nathaniel arrived at the same time as the police. He grabbed Ivy in a tight hug, trying to calm her down. Her sobs could be heard by the crowd of people now gathering in the hallway. He felt a semblance of relief when he finally saw Anthony push his way through.

"What do you need from me, sir?" Anthony was ex military and was always about business.

"Clear this floor. Relocate all employees to the lower level and have them either share office space or use the conference rooms. I want this whole level locked down. If they work for Mrs. Wallace, I want them gone."

"Yes, sir." Anthony turned to his men and gave out orders. Soon, he saw the crowd being dispersed and felt Ivy relax a little.

"Excuse me. My name's detective Blem. I'll be heading up this case. I'm going to need to ask you a few questions Mrs. Wallace."

Ivy tensed up in his arms, but found the courage to turn to the detective. Nathaniel shoved a wad of tissue in her hands and she dabbed her runny nose. She looked up at him and thanked him.

"Mrs. Wallace, we can sit over here," the detective said, motioning towards the white leather couch.

Ivy nodded and made her way over. When she sat down, Nate sat beside her and slid his arm around her shoulders. His support was so comforting that she eased a little closer to him.

Detective Blem sat in a chair across from them. His appearance seemed laid back and uninterested, but his eyes told another story. They seemed to take everything in all at once. Sharp and intelligent. She could tell he was good at his job.

"Mrs. Wallace, I'll ask a few questions and you can respond any way you like. But please, tell me everything. It makes things a lot easier for me when it's time to do the paperwork," he said with a smile.

"Alright."

"Good. Now, you called in a little over an hour ago asking for an ambulance to be sent here, correct?"

"Yes. My sister got cut. She was bleeding so much. I didn't know what to do."

"How did she get cut?"

"Glass from the table," she said, nodding towards the now destroyed table.

Detective Blem didn't even glance over to the table. He kept his eyes on Ivy. "Can you tell me how she ended up with a piece of the glass in her side?"

Ivy nodded. It all seemed so unreal to her. "We were fighting and we both fell on the table. I got up thinking she was going to hit me again, and that's when I saw the blood."

"So you both fell on the table?"

"Yes."

"But you're not cut, right?"

"No. Why does that matter?"

"Be careful detective Blem," said Nate, staring at the man in anger.

"Just doing my job Mr. Wallace. Sorry if it seems rude or blunt." When Nathaniel didn't respond, the detective turned back to Ivy and continued.

"Is this your office?"

"No. This is June's office."

"Why were you here?"

Ivy glanced at Nate for a moment before answering. "I came to speak with her about something. But we started to argue."

"What did you speak about?" Detective Blem had leaned back a little and looked bored out his mind. However, he was soaking in everything about Ivy. Her posture, her breathing, her expression, tone of voice. Everything. He needed facts and he was a genius at reading people.

Ivy looked down at her hands nervously. She knew that she would have to tell everything, but knew that it would involve Nate. When she glanced at Nate, he nodded his approval.

"I came to fire her."

*Now we're getting somewhere.* "Now why would you

need to fire your sister?" he asked nonchalantly.

She took a deep breath to settle her nerves and then looked the detective in the eyes. "My sister tried to ruin my marriage. A few days ago, she drugged my husband and had him placed in bed with some woman. But, she came clean about it this morning when I accused her and we argued over it. I told her she was fired, and she became angry and charged at me. We started fighting and then we fell onto the table. You know the rest."

Blem turned to look at Nathaniel. "This woman she placed you in bed with. Do you know her? Do you know where we can find her?"

"No. I don't know her. I was drugged. I woke up to my wife screaming at me and then I went home to beg her forgiveness."

Blem looked at them both and smiled. He had a feeling they weren't telling him everything. "So how do you know your sister was the one to drug you?" When neither of them answered he shook his head. "Listen, you can hold back all the secrets you want. But, if your sister dies, you're looking at murder. And either way, I'll get my answers."

Nathaniel felt Ivy shudder beside him. The detective was using his scare tactics and he could tell they were affecting her. At that moment Anthony walked over and handed Nathaniel a disc.

"Sorry for interrupting, but I thought you'd want to see this," he said in his no-nonsense tone.

"What's this," asked Nate eyeing the disc.

"It's the footage from the security cameras. Every

higher management office has them. After Mr. Morgan's suicide attempt, we had them installed for insurance reasons."

"I would like to see that footage," said Blem.

Anthony walked over to the hidden cabinet and pressed on a flat board. A panel slid across revealing a forty inch flat screen television and entertainment center. He powered on the unit and then slid the disc inside. He then used the remote to fast forward to the time when Ivy entered June's office.

Everyone watched in silence as the whole incident played before them. Ivy flinched beside him when she saw how they fell onto the table. She turned away from the sight of the blood and he could understand why. It was gruesome even to him.

Once the scene played out fully, Anthony stopped the disc and handed it to the detective. "This copy is for you, sir. We have our own copy." He then turned to Ivy. "I had your car sent home Mrs. Wallace. I'm sure you'd like to ride home with Mr. Wallace."

Ivy nodded. "Yes, thank you Anthony."

Anthony nodded and walked back over to the door. He wouldn't leave the office until all the police and their staff was gone.

"Well, I guess that's all I need then," said Blem tucking the disc in his inside jacket pocket. He got to his feet and glanced over at Ivy. "I do have one question though."

"And what's that?" asked Nate.

Blem looked directly at Ivy. "Based on what I saw in the video, your sister clearly attacked you with the intent to do harm. Will you be filing charges against her?"

"What? No, of course not. This was all an accident," said Ivy flustered.

Blem stared at her for a long moment and then smiled. "Okay. If I have any more questions, I'll give you a call. But, I'm pretty sure I won't need to."

He started towards the door, then stopped. "Oh. Your sister was taken to Sullivan Hospital. Thought you'd like to know that." And with that last bit of information he was gone.

Nathaniel leaned over and kissed Ivy on top of her head. "Come on. Let's get you to the hospital. I know you're worried about her."

"Yes, and thank you."

"For what?" he asked, pulling her to her feet.

"For not giving up Terri's name. I didn't want to rat her out after helping us get back together. It just didn't seem right."

"No. It didn't. Come on, let's get out of here."

# Chapter 18

At the hospital Ivy and Nathaniel was asked to wait inside the green room while June was rushed into surgery. The procedure took four hours, but the nurse assured Ivy everything would be okay. Ivy hated hospitals. She believed that all the staff was trained to give you vague answers to your questions all the while showing you their sick blank smile.

"Why is it taking so long?" she repeated again. Ivy had been asking that same question to no one in particular for the past two hours. She stood up and walked over to the window, peering into the late afternoon sunshine.

"Relax Ivy. Dr. Darby is here now and I'm sure he's doing everything he can for June. It shouldn't be much longer."

No sooner had the words left his mouth that Dr. Darby walked through the yellow double swinging doors looking tired. The only thing that kept Ivy from worrying was the smile on his lips. He joined Nathaniel and Ivy near the window.

"Mr. And Mrs. Wallace. I'm happy to say that your sister's surgery went through without a hitch. She was lucky that none of her arteries had been cut during the fall. It was a clean cut. She required stitches on the inside. Not many," he said when he saw Ivy blanch. "Just a few. She lost a lot of blood, but she's stable now. She pulled through remarkably."

"Can I see her?" Ivy asked in a hushed tone. Her nerves have been running on high since she'd woke up that morning.

"You can go in, but she won't know you're there. She's been heavily sedated. It's a precaution to keep her from tearing her stitches. But, I'll allow a quick visit."

Ivy gave him a soft smile. "Thank you Dr. Darby."

"It's not a problem," he said smiling warmly. He turned to leave, but stopped as if he had something else to say. "Oh, I almost forgot. We have a hospital counselor who comes by and visits the patients. After a brief discussion with detective Blem, I gave her the green light to go and visit with June in the morning. Her names Dr. Weaver. It's standard procedure."

"I think that's a good idea," said Nathaniel. When Ivy looked up at him surprised, he took her hand in his. "In light of everything that's happened these past couple of days. It might do her some good to talk to someone," he said, reminding her of what June had done.

"You're right." She looked back to Dr. Darby. "I'd like to see her now."

"Right this way," he said, and proceeded down

the hallway with them following. He stopped in front of a door and pushed it open. The soft swoosh and beeps of the machines surrounding June caused Ivy to catch her breath in apprehension.

Sensing her anxiety, Dr. Darby tried to reassure her. "Don't worry about all the machines. Most are there just to monitor her."

Ivy nodded and moved towards the bed. Her eyes filled with tears as she looked down at June laying so still.

"I can only allow a few minutes. I'll be waiting outside at the nurses station."

As Dr. Darby made his exit, Nathaniel moved closer to Ivy. "She's going to be alright Ivy. You heard what the doctor said."

"I know," she said, shaking her head. "It's just hard to understand why she did any of this."

"And that's another reason why seeing that counselor is a good idea. Maybe she can get some answers from her."

Ivy leaned down and placed a kiss on June forehead. She pulled the hair from her face and tucked it behind her ear. "I can't stay June, but I'll be here for you in the morning. I promise," she whispered before a sob slid from her lips.

Nathaniel pulled Ivy into his arms and held her tightly, rubbing her back comforting her. "Shh, it's okay baby. She's going to be fine. But, you're going to have to be strong for her okay?"

Ivy nodded against his chest. "I know. I will. She needs me now." Everything that happened before their fight would need to be put on hold, because right now, all that Ivy cared about was June getting better. Regardless of what they went through, she would always be her sister.

"Come on. Let me take you home," said Nathaniel, pulling her from the room.

****

The rest of the day went by in a blur for Ivy. She had been nervous about making the call to their parents. They were away on a trip to Rome and her mother said they wouldn't be cutting their trip short and returning any time soon. It bothered Ivy that they wouldn't end their trip to come see about June, but maybe it was for the best. June and their parents never got along. It was a situation that Ivy never could quite understand. They would only upset her and maybe worsen her condition.

Later that day, Ivy made calls to her senior managers at her company, making sure things were running smoothly in her and June's absence. She knew people at the company would talk, but she didn't care about that. Her only concern was seeing that June got better and figuring out what to do next about the whole issue.

Before long, the sun had been chased away by the moon, and Ivy was lying in bed trying to force her mind to slow down so she could get some sleep. She'd eaten very little at dinner and she could see that Nate was beginning to worry. The only thing that had calmed her down a little was calling the hospital to check up on June. She was told that her condition was still stable and she was still resting.

Hearing the water go off in the bathroom, she leaned over and turned off the lamp on her bedside table. She heard the door when it opened and listened to Nate moving around the room. She lay there with her back to him as she gazed out the window. She'd left the curtains open so she could look out at the stars.

Nate climbed in the bed after he dried off. He slid up behind Ivy and kissed her shoulder. Thinking she was asleep, he rolled over onto his back, releasing an exhausted sigh.

Ivy was relaxed, yet her mind wouldn't let her drift off. Something June said had been running through her mind over and over making her feel restless. *"He was inside of me just as much as he was inside of you."* That statement had cut her like a knife. And even though Terri had cleared things up, and she and Nate had made up, she still had to ask.

"Honey, I need to ask you something," she said, breaking the peaceful quiet in the room.

"Go ahead, but if it's about you pressing charges, I think instead you should seek help for your sister. I know she attacked you, but jail isn't going to do her any good."

"I thought about that too, but that wasn't what I was going to ask you," she said turning to face him. The light from the moon illuminated the room just enough so she could see his eyes in the dark. They both were now facing each other. Their bodies brushing against each other under the cool sheets.

"Well, go ahead baby. Ask away," Nate said, lightly brushing his fingers across her cheeks.

Ivy was beginning to second guess asking him, but knew this was the only way she could get some kind of closure on the matter.

"June said that the two of you had sex." She was surprised at how calm she sounded, because inside she was wound as tight as a knot.

Nate pulled back from her offended. "Are you asking me or are you accusing me?" he asked hurt by the accusation.

"No im not accusing you, I'm asking you. I didn't mean for it to sound like I was accusing you. I just needed to ask."

Nate sighed loudly, seeming tired of all the lies and mistrust. "Baby, that woman is trying to send you to the crazy house with her. Think about it Ivy. If I was sleeping with her, then why did she hire Terri to try and make me cheat on you? If I was sleeping with her like she claimed, she could have just told you I was sleeping with her. She wouldn't have needed to involve anyone else," he said, sounding annoyed that Ivy would even go there.

Ivy thought about what Nathaniel said and agreed that June was making her feel insecure. "You're right. I'm sorry for letting her get in my head. It's just been a lot going on lately, and I guess im really tired of it all."

Nate reached out and tucked a wayward curl behind her ear. "It's alright. I understand that this is hard for you, and I'm sorry she put you through this.

But none of it is true Ivy. Trust me. You're all I'll ever want in a woman. Just you," he said, brushing his thumb lightly across her bottom lip.

Once Nathaniel voiced his views about June's claim, Ivy shook the thought of them two sleeping together from her mind. He made it sound so ridiculous after what he said about her hiring Terri. Deciding to just leave the subject alone, she broached the subject of June's condition.

"I've decided that I don't want to press any charges on her," she said switching the topic. "Maybe getting her some help will be the best thing for her. I just wanted her to stay out of our lives. I didn't want for any of this to happen."

Her voice sounded a little wobbly, so Nathaniel pulled her in his arms. She curled up against his side holding onto him for dear life. Nathaniel smoothed down her hair while whispering soft words to her. Soon, he felt her body relax against his as she dozed off.

Nathaniel smiled coldly into the darkness of the room as he held Ivy close. He'd made the mistake of sleeping with June on numerous occasions for financial benefits. There were a few perks other than the money. June was wild in bed and would do just about anything to please him. He would never have chosen her to wed, and instead he'd chosen the inexperienced Ivy. No, June was great in bed, but there were too many things about her that didn't please him.

For one, June was extremely jealous of Ivy. He

noticed that the first night he met them on the cruise. Then she fucked up her chance at getting into political office by getting caught sleeping with the Mayor's son. Besides that, she wasn't rich. It was pathetic that she worked for her little sister, who was obscenely rich. Nathaniel shook his head. *Why mess with the help when you could fuck with the boss?* He laughed silently at his private joke.

If he could have combined the two of them, he would have, but since he had to choose, he wisely chose the money. His plan was to continue sleeping with June whenever he wanted to. However, knowing that she killed her first husband had him withdrawing from her. *You can't trust a bitch like that.*

Somewhere she lost a few screws. She went behind his back and came up with that foolish plan of hiring that Vows bitch to get him caught cheating so Ivy would divorce him. *Hell, I'm not about to lose everything just for a piece of good ass.*

He sighed heavily and shook his head, snuggling closer against his wife. *Everything was working out until June began to demand more of me,* he thought silently to himself.

"I love you, Nathaniel," Ivy whispered sleepily, her lips pressing against his chest.

*These bitches always want more...*he thought, before he responded with, "I love you too sweetie. Always," he whispered, his eyes peering coldly into the darkness.

# Chapter 19

Terri sat on the balcony of the hotel suite overlooking the white sandy beach in Aruba. She and Malik decided that they needed a vacation after the last case with June Foster. She just didn't know that he wanted to take that vacation together.

Now she sat smiling as she sipped her virgin Long Island Ice Tea, happy that her drink was now the only virgin in her life. She looked back inside the room and saw her man still sound asleep. *My man.* Her smile widened.

Making love had been more than she had ever imagined. Malik was experienced, gentle, and attentive to her body. It had been so good that Terri had the notion to head back in there and wake him up for round four.

*Why not?* She took one last sip from her drink and padded barefoot over to the bed. When she looked down at Malik's naked body her inner kitty purred to life and she clenched her muscles enhancing the sweet ache. He was lying on his back, and all that he had been blessed with was standing at attention. *I think I'll take that as an invitation.*

Terri slid out of Malik's shirt and climb on top of

him straddling his thighs. She marveled at the tight muscles of his torso that were covered by the dark ink of artistic tattoo's. Lightly trailing her fingers down his stomach, she didn't stop until she touched his dick. She loved the smooth, velvety surface around it and the hardness beneath.

Massaging the crown with her thumb, she lifted her hips and felt him ease between her moist lips. She rotated her hips, letting his stiffness glide back and forth over her clit. Her soft moans were her own aphrodisiac.

Feeling herself getting lost, she eased up a bit more, and allowed him to invade her in a way no man ever had. She paused only for a moment to allow her body to adjust to his thickness. *Damn, he was thick. So fucking thick,* she thought as she concentrated on her breathing.

Once she felt her walls relax, and then flex around him, she knew she was ready to take in more. She released her thigh muscles and pressed down. The feeling of Malik's body merging with hers, claiming her, was like a delicious melody being played inside her.

Not able to hold back any longer, she leaned back and grasped his knees. Lifting all the way to the tip, she twirled her hips slowly before tightening her inner walls and pressing back down. The sensation was so unbelievable and amazing that she hurried to do it again.

Over and over she lifted, twirled, and reclaimed his dick, always clamping her muscles. When the tension began to build she stopped, trying desperately to hold out for a more intense orgasm.

"Don't stop. Keep going."

The sound of Malik's voice had her looking up to meet his eyes. His gaze was dark and focused. His breathing just as ragged as her own.

"Touch yourself Terri. I want to watch you please your body."

Feeling a little self conscious, she stared down at him through half closed lids.

"Like this," he said, and proceeded to reach down to where their bodies joined. His fingers began to stroke her clit through the tiny patch of hair shaped in a star. "I love that design you have down there, baby. It's so damn sexy."

He continued to massage her pussy, all the while staring into her eyes. "Now you," he said, reaching for her hand.

Terri gave him her hand and let him place it between her legs. He guided her fingers over her, sliding back and forth. Applying pressure when he felt she needed it.

"Now move baby. Just like you were before."

Immediately Terri began to lift, twirl, and reclaim his dick.

"Mmm, yesss. Just like that Terri." After helping her for a few minutes, he soon released her hand and sat back to watch.

The woman on top of him was a total opposite of the shy woman that had walked into the hotel with him hours ago. This woman wanted pleasure and knew how to claim it. And she knew how to draw it out of him to get it.

Malik watched in awe as Terri rode him like a veteran. She rocked and dipped, picked up speed, and slowed down at just the right times. Her breast were perfectly round with small perky nipples that he loved taking into his mouth. Everything about her was sexy, right down to her plump ass that he now held in his hands.

"Come on, baby. Stay with me. Don't give in. Hold it until you can't hold it any longer," Malik said, as he began rising up to meet her.

Their moans and sighs filled the room merging with the loud crashes of the waves against the rocks. Terri was still massaging her clit, and Malik eyes were glued to her. Feeling a quiver in her lower stomach, she tried to slow down, but it wasn't working.

"Malik, I can't," she said breathlessly.

"Yes, you can. Keep going. Ride this dick baby."

Malik began digging in deeper, determined to push her over the edge. His shaft was buried deep within her and she was taking his length like a pro. Suddenly, her nails dug into his leg and she cried out.

"Oh, shitttt!"

Terri's body gave way to her orgasm and every fiber of her being clamped down on Malik's dick. She was able to lift one last time before the room started to spin and her head fell backwards. The hand that was pleasuring her clit moved up to pinch her nipple driving her more insane.

Watching her erotic dance above him was more than he could have imagined. She was lost in her own world of enjoyment and he felt privileged to watch it. Not wanting to be left behind, Malik sat up and wrapped both arms around her waist holding her tightly to him. Once he felt that she couldn't get away from him, he began to rock into her with strong deep strokes.

Terri squirmed to get away, but couldn't move. Her clit was brushing against his torso, giving her the sweetest sensations as he ground his dick masterfully into her. She was trapped by his hold and was unable to stop the second orgasm from rolling through her.

She wrapped her arms around his neck and buried her face into her arm. All she could do was hold on for dear life as wave after wave of powerful tremors began to physically torture her body, mind, and soul.

"Malik, Malik, Malik…"

She chanted his name unable to say anything else. When she felt his body finally tense and give way to his own release, she silently thanked God, for she didn't know how much more she could take.

Malik's body tightened, and then jerked, as he continuously bucked beneath her. He felt as though he was shattering into millions of pieces, but was still able to feel her touch. Never in his life had he felt such a total connection with a woman. Never. Until now.

Feeling drained and unbelievably sated, he lifted his head to look at Terri. The satisfied and peaceful expression on her face filled his heart and his ego.

He knew this was it. That there would be no other after her. He knew it before he even walked into the hotel. *I've always known it.*

Malik leaned down and kissed her tenderly on her lips, savoring her taste. "This is it for me, Terri."

Terri drew back to look up at him. "What do you mean?"

"I mean there's not going to be anyone after you," he said, moving a damp curl from her cheek.

Terri smiled, then leaned in for a kiss. When she had enough, she pulled away, breathing heavy.

"As if you had a choice," she said smiling.

Malik shook his head, laughing. He grabbed her by the waist and they tumbled to the mattress already deep in another kiss.

# Epilogue

June Foster sat in her pristine white room at the Blue Hill Mental Complex staring through the tiny square that they called a window. She had been doped up on Ritalin since Judge Perkins, who just happened to be a close friend of Nathaniel's, had her admitted. She remembered looking over at Ivy sitting there across the table in the pristine conference room with tears running down her face as she signed the papers that her lawyer slid over to her.

"Ivy." Saying her name out loud kept June feeling. Kept her focused.

"Nathaniel." She let his name roll from her lips on a soft caress. "My Nathaniel."

With a smile on her face, she closed her eyes, remembering the feel of his touch. The way his mouth slanted across hers before his tongue would invade it. Her hand reached up and she slid her fingers over her lips. With her back to the door, she eased the pill from her mouth, letting it drop onto her lap. *That makes twenty two pills I've saved.*

June sighed loudly, then turned back to her work. She sat with her art pad open on her desk drawing stick figures of three people. The drawing was of her, her husband and their little girl. She had taken the time to name each person with a caption over their head. Nathaniel, June, and our baby girl May.

*Soon my love. Soon we will be together again and start our very own family.* She picked up her yellow crayon and began to draw a sun.

Dr. Charles Johnson stood looking in the glass window outside her room evaluating her behavior. June had been placed here now going on four months, and as far as he'd seen, had no violent behavior. However, according to her record, she was prone to showing a rage and strength far beyond what her small stature should allow.

*That's not the June I know*, he said as he watched her draw.

"How long have you been giving her Ritalin?" he asked the doctor standing beside him. Dr. Chessfield looked fresh out of school and Charles knew the man child was intimidated by him.

"Uhhh, I believe only a few weeks," he said sounding unsure.

Charles turned away from June to look down at him. "Are you sure it's only been a few weeks?" he asked sharply.

Dr. Chessfield swallowed numerous times as he opened June's chart. "I'm not sure. I've just been assigned to her a couple of days ago and I haven't had the chance to go through her file yet," he said trying to scan through the papers.

Becoming disgusted with the man's lack of

professionalism, Charles held out his hand. "Let me have the file doctor. I'll have a look, if you don't mind."

Dr. Chessfield smiled appreciatively. "Thank you, Dr. Johnson. I must admit, I've been feeling a little overwhelmed lately with the added workload I received. As if I didn't have enough already," he said, trying to make a joke, but coming off sounded pathetic.

"Don't worry about it," said Charles, using the man's weakness to his advantage. "How about I help out starting with this patient here. I'll meet you back downstairs in say," he stopped to check his watch, "two hours. We can have lunch together and discuss the patients."

Dr. Chessfield beamed his smile at Charles. "Wow! That would be great Dr. Johnson," he said, shoving his wire rim glasses further up on his nose. "I'll see you downstairs in two hours."

He turned and walked away with a little more pep in his step. Charles shook his head. *Stupid fool just gave me his patient's chart knowing damn well he's not supposed to do that no matter who the hell I am.*

Shrugging his shoulders, he swiped his access card to open June's room door. She didn't even turn around to acknowledge him in the room. Charles closed the door and approached her. He then sat on the only other chair in the room. He glanced down at her drawing frowning at what he saw.

Cautiously, he reached over and pulled the crayon from her hand and tossed it on the desk. He dragged her chair around to face him and leaned in close to her face. Her eyes were cast down to her lap.

"Look at me June," he said in an even tone. When she didn't respond, he lifted his hand and slapped her hard across her face. "Cut the crap June and look at me!"

June's head lifted quickly and anger glittered hot and fierce in her eyes.

"Ahh, there you are." He grabbed his pen light and shined it in her eyes. He then leaned back and smiled. "You can stop acting now. I can see that your eyes are clear, and you're not sedated."

When she only sat there glaring at him, he laughed.

"So, your little plan backfired and it landed your ass in here. The man you've been chasing called in a favor to have you tucked away so that he can live his life in peace without you stalking him."

"You don't know what you're talking about," she hissed.

Charles laughed, but quickly got serious. "I know what you were doing, June. Dammit, what's so damn great about the guy anyway? All he ever wanted was her money and to fuck you. I would have given you anything," he said frustrated. "Why couldn't you be satisfied with a man like me?"

June sat there looking at him. Different emotions were rolling through her like a storm. Suddenly, her eyes watered and she licked her dry lips. "It's because he belongs to her. She's always gotten everything she wanted. Everything!" she yelled trembling.

"I never got anything. No attention from our parents. None of the boys in school ever wanted to be my boyfriend. They all just wanted to fuck," she said angrily. "Oh, but little Ms. Princess got it all. She even got him."

Charles looked at her as if he was seeing her for the first time. All this time he thought June was acting like a bitch out of spite, but now he saw that she was only lashing out from being ignored and feeling jealous. What he saw was a woman needing to be loved. Not a psychotic patient.

"June. Do you love him? Be honest. Do you love him, or do you want him just because he belongs to Ivy?"

June was breathing heavy and her hands were gripping the arms of her chair tightly. Her body ached with the need to lash out, but somehow she couldn't. She couldn't do that to Charles. Not after that night. *That night.*

"Answer me, dammit!" he demanded yanking her chair.

"I want him because he's hers," she growled as a tear rolled down her cheek.

Charles leaned back and smiled. "That's what I thought. You don't love him. You never loved him. You just want your sister to suffer. To hurt like you do."

When she didn't respond, only sat there letting tear after tear roll down her face, he reached over to dry them with his thumb.

"So, how about you leave his sorry ass alone, and be with a man that knows how to care for you, and definitely knows how to satisfy you. Then, once I get you clear of here, we can decide together about dishing out a world of hurt to that sister of yours."

June closed her eyes briefly and then opened them. "And why would you do that for me," she asked almost afraid to hear his answer.

Charles looked away for a moment and then back to her. "Because I care for you June. More than I should," he said sincerely. "Also, a long time ago I was feeling exactly the way you're feeling. I had an older sister who couldn't do no wrong in my parents' eyes. Needles to say she was a down low hell raiser and I got blamed for most of the shit she did."

Intrigued, June eased closer to him. "What did you do?"

"Me? Nothing. But its ashamed that her boyfriend overdosed on prom night and flipped his car over killing them both. So sad," he said, smiling coldly.

June gave him her first genuine smile. "So sad indeed."

Charles leaned across at a snail's pace until he was able to rest his lips on hers. June sat still at first, but then she allowed herself to let go, and relaxed against him. Their kiss, although brief, wiped away any lingering doubts between them. As they drew apart, June exhaled her warm breath against her own fingers.

"Finally," she said reflectively.

"Finally," said Charles, repeating the softly spoken

word.

Charles sat there thinking of how long it would take to get her released, because he knew that this wasn't the last the world would hear from June Foster.

# What's next for Angel B?

www.ingramcontent.com/pod-product-compliance
Lightning Source LLC
Chambersburg PA
CBHW061153170626
46809CB00003B/1076